THE BRIGHTEST STAR

Rennie was a mining engineer in South Africa and a very competent one; but of course she came up against a lot of opposition on account of her sex, and the latest critic in a long line was Todd Dillman. Did her job *really* make her less feminine? Rennie didn't think so—especially when she considered the way she felt about Todd . . .

THE BRIGHTEST
STAR

BY

ROUMELIA LANE

MILLS & BOON LIMITED
17–19 FOLEY STREET
LONDON W1A 1DR

First published 1978
Philippine copyright 1978
This edition 1978

© Roumelia Lane 1978

ISBN 0 263 72590 1

Set in Linotype Plantin 10 on 11 pt.

Made and printed in Great Britain by
Richard Clay (The Chaucer Press), Ltd., Bungay, Suffolk

CHAPTER ONE

RENNIE flung the wrench from her oil-smeared hands in a burst of feminine frustration. In the first place she didn't know why an expensive bulldozer should suddenly break down, and in the second she wasn't sure it couldn't be better dealt with by one of the native boy mechanics. Carelessly wiping the beads of moisture from her brow, she stood and squinted at the view.

She was a youthful twenty-two with a forthright blue gaze and a generous mouth. Her dark hair, which was shot with plum-coloured lights when the sun caught it, was stuffed under a grubby peaked cap. Dungarees, their colour dubious beneath the oil and grease stains, sagged unbecomingly on her slim frame.

Shielding her eyes from the glare with her hand, she could make out the view which was becoming increasingly familiar to her; the company town with its white houses and gardens and farms sprawling over the lion-coloured slopes and the steely glint of the double fence of barbed wire which ran for miles enclosing the Kramer diamond mine compound.

It was less than a week since she had flown out from London and taken the train up from Pretoria to this little-known area in the Northern Transvaal. She had soon discovered that the mining settlement, located near a hamlet called Vukasi from which it derived its name and close to two fairly sizeable towns, Tombaza and Wykveld, was vastly different from the city with its avenues of blossoming jacarandas and sidewalks flanked by imposing shops and offices. This was Africa, wild and rugged with endless miles of bushveld under a brilliant sky, the Africa of animals and live things scurrying unseen in the shimmering distance.

Her roaming gaze latched on to something which brought a pucker of annoyance to her already furrowed brow. Oh no, not visitors! Not now! The two figures on horseback were indistinguishable as they crossed the grassy wastes outside the barbed wire, but there was no doubt by their leisurely pace that they were heading this way.

Rennie was greasing the blade linkage of the bulldozer and concentrating hard when a few minutes later a voice called out, 'Hello! How's the work going?'

She looked up to see a girl with straight reddish-gold hair and good features astride an impetuous black stallion.

'I'm finding it quite absorbing,' Rennie replied politely. She had already met Lila Harwood with the heavy-lidded sardonic gaze and bored smile at the mine manager's house and found nothing in the girl to warm to.

'There you are, Todd!' Lila's crisp, high-pitched tones rang out laughingly now. 'You said you wouldn't believe it till you saw it with your own eyes. Well, here she is—our very first woman engineer!' She informed Rennie cheerfully, 'I've been telling my friends about you. Todd here was sceptical, so I brought him along to see for himself.'

'I'm flattered to have attracted so much attention.' Rennie met the green glance of the man on the second horse. He had a wide laconic mouth and a wide brow over which his thick hair lay in a clipped, neat style. In fact he was all width. His shoulders filled the suedeskin windcheater which he wore over spotless riding breeches.

'Todd Dillman has a house close to the airstrip,' Lila made the introduction. 'He's a countryman of yours.'

'Hardly,' came a voice deep and lazy. 'I've been here ten years.' Todd Dillman allowed a noticeable pause, then added drily, 'They weren't producing pint-sized greasemonkeys when I was in England.'

'You'd be surprised what we women get up to nowadays,' Rennie cooed, investigating the scooping mechanism of the bulldozer. After four years in the business she was used to the leg-pulling from the so-called superior male, but something in the way this man eyed her grubby overalls and oil-smudged cheeks ruffled her none too steady calm. Laying it on thick, she added, 'We even have lady sea captains now, you know.'

'Heaven help the Navy!' The laconic mouth sloped at one corner.

Rennie rummaged in her tool box. 'I take it you don't agree with equal rights for women, Mr Dillman?' She met his gaze sweetly. 'Could it be that you're afraid we might improve things?'

'I doubt it.' His grin was tight and at a mocking slant. 'The only thing I ever saw a woman improve was a packet of trouble.'

'Oh, come now, Miss ... Bernie ... Bennie ...'

'The name's Rennie.' She had almost forgotten Lila Harwood on the restive stallion.

'That's right. I knew it was something quaint.' Lila, who was probably a few years older than herself, looked amused and went on, 'Africa is a man's world. You'll have a hard time convincing the types around here that your ability is any match for theirs.'

'I've no intention of trying,' Rennie replied flatly. She thought that with this the company would drift off, but as she tossed oily rags to left and right from the depths of her tool box, Todd Dillman, in aggravatingly relaxed pose astride his chestnut steed, asked, 'What's gone wrong with the shiny mechanical shovel here? Don't tell me it's broken down already?'

'It's probably only the locking nut dislocated by vibration,' Rennie said knowledgeably, wondering what business it was of his. Beneath the scoop, jammed in mid-air, she searched vainly for another retaining nut. If only she could lay her hands on what she wanted, just once! But it was always the same. As a student she had never been able to keep a tidy tool box like the other trainee engineers. She always worked like a distracted artist, tossing pliers and spanners around like discarded paint tubes, so that in no time things became a jumble.

Only too aware that the man on horseback was ironically making the most of her incompetence, she looked up and flashed in honeyed tones, 'And what do *you* do for a living, Mr Dillman?'

'I'm a landscape architect,' he replied with lazy assurance while he pointedly watched her fumble.

'He's re-designing the grounds of Rosedale,' Lila put in peaceably. 'Giving a face lift to over twenty-seven acres of garden.'

Rosedale, the Harwood residence on the road out of Vukasi? Yes, Rennie had seen it. Who could miss it? A grand Dutch-style manor, walled in and aloof.

'So you grow flowers for an occupation,' she purred at the man in the saddle. 'How ingenious!' Then fishing out the nut she had been searching for she felt sufficiently bolstered to smile nettlingly, 'Well, if this is a man's world I don't think I have much to worry about.'

Lila's horse was playing up, and clearly losing interest in the Kramer diamond mine's new engineer, she said with a certain brittle sparkle, 'We're taking a ride out to the south boundary. It's a lovely day and I'm in the mood for a fast gallop.'

'Don't let me keep you.' Rennie studied the angle of the jammed scoop.

The stallion was steered away from the barbed wire. As he turned to follow, Todd Dillman, having lost none of his air of superiority, remarked with an idle gleam, 'A simple job like that. You'll have it fixed in no time, I bet.'

He cantered off and Rennie watched him go, but not without a whipped up feeling of satisfaction. Blow for blow she reckoned she had shown him she was more than a match for his sniping humour.

Capable and at ease in the saddle, he caught up with his companion and with her eyes still on the pale, wind-cheatered width of him Rennie found herself wondering what his relationship was with the lovely, insensitive Lila Harwood. He worked in the grounds where she lived, so it was fairly certain that they saw a lot of each other. Perhaps they were something more than just friends?

Turning away, she re-applied herself to the job in hand. Why waste time figuring out what didn't concern her anyway? Todd Dillman didn't come into her work sphere.

Carefully holding the sticky, greased nut in her hand, she hunted around for a suitable length of wood. It was no easy task propping up the bulldozer blade to the level of the loose bolt, in fact she knew it was a highly dangerous one to attempt on her own. Yet she pushed and heaved, working with a dogged determination and a prolonged surge of strength which surprised her, hammering and coaxing the bolt into line and finally anchoring the nut into place.

Limp and exhausted when the thing was done, she climbed up top nevertheless with a victorious light in her blue eyes, swinging the huge-tyred wheels over the sandy ground and flicking the levers as though it was child's play. She didn't know why, but the thought of the rugged-looking landscape architect passing back this way and noticing that the bulldozer was once again in working order somehow made her day.

She drove across the limitless space, its surface resembling the craters of the moon. Mining methods at the Kramer diamond mine were the open-cast quarrying kind and littered over the grey-blue surface which lay like an open wound in the midst of the rolling, golden veld, hydraulic excavators, bulldozers and earth-moving machines worked to expose the diamondiferous gravels.

Close at hand were the treatment and recovery plants and beyond, in the dust-clouded distance on a flat stretch, she could see the rooftops of the workers' compound. Here were the hostels of the African labour force plus streets, stores, a cinema and workshops, all within the barbed wire circumference. Here too was her own modest accommodation, a two-roomed house with the primary essentials and its own patch of lawn. But it would be many hours yet before she could retreat to it. As usual the thought of the work ahead filled her with a deep depression.

She left the giant bulldozer on the edge of the quarrying area to be picked up by one of the Basuto drivers and took to the mine truck she used for covering the work site. Before she reached the section where the drag-line was in operation she knew that things were not going as well as they should. The monster, with a boom over a hundred feet long from which the drag-line bucket was slung, could pick up more than six tons of ore at each bite. At the moment it was retrieving less than half the load.

'I thought Mr Bonell got to the bottom of the trouble yesterday, Abraham?' Leaving the truck, she addressed the quarry foreman, whose rolling brown eyes were viewing the jerking cable nervously.

'Baas was here, then he go away again,' he shrugged his gangling frame on which flopped the company's blue overalls. 'Very bad—twisted cable.'

'I'll have a word with him.' Tight-mouthed, Rennie swung back to the truck. In a cloud of dust she slewed over to the nearest phone post. With the whining of the machines and the roar of tumbling earth it was always difficult to get any sense out of these things, but sticking at it she finally got through.

There was no mistaking the thick, slurring voice which greeted her jovially over the line, then went on to enquire, 'How goes it, honey?'

'Leith, the bucket excavator's fouling up again. It's three days since I reported it to your office.' Rennie's tones were firm.

In contrast the reply came over easily. 'Sure, but I got other things, you know.'

Like what? she wanted to ask grimly. Tinkering with your motor-bike in the toolsheds and looking in on the card games among the off-shift workers? Instead she said, 'I thought you were going to do an overhaul?'

The voice became a little offhand. 'You take it, kid. You'll find all you need to know in the textbooks.'

'I have no authority to disrupt production,' Rennie answered crossly. 'You're the chief engineer, and if this thing continues much longer'—brutally she trained the ear-piece towards the sound of the grinding cables—'you're liable to have a full-scale breakdown on your hands.'

There was a pause. 'In that case I suppose I'd better come over.' A peevish note mingled with the geniality, then the line went dead.

Ten minutes later Rennie stood in the path of the braking jeep. The man who climbed out was a burly six-footer with a mop of unruly curls and a sluggish, carefree manner which belied his experience. His smile was disarming as ever in his fleshy, misshapen face as he met Rennie. 'Now what's the beef, youngster? I can't be in three places at once, you understand that, don't you?'

There was the smell of liquor on his breath, but Rennie went along with the explanation. She told him earnestly, 'I've examined the crane-shaft feed above the cabin. I'm worried about the friction of the anchor wheel. It smells hot.'

'Well, if it's as serious as that we'd better take a look.' Cheerfully he went to investigate the trouble.

His huge hands wielding a mighty wrench, jokingly uncouth as he larked with the African mine diggers, he tackled the complicated machinery on the railed-in platform above the cabin. Leith was a first-class engineer, but prone as he was to drink and the comforts of his bunk, she wondered how he had managed to hold down his job for so long.

She stayed to assist with the dismantling until a message came to say that there was a blockage in the separation plant. From here she was called to check on a faulty roller on one of the recovery plant grease belts.

The sun was an orange orb silhouetting the fretwork of thorn trees and acacias against its spreading glow when she finally drove back to the residential section and dumped the truck and her tool box in the shed adjoining the engineer's office. This was the time of day she liked best. This was when she didn't mind Africa with its foreign feel and its awesome sense of space.

In the softening light the veld surrounding the workers' compound was a tawny tapestry broken by clumps of bush wistaria and the starry white of wild pear. The air was laced with the earth's scents laid bare by stirring breezes and cicadas whirred musically in the long grasses.

Rennie peeled off her cap and overalls and in linen slacks and checked shirt she washed off the oil and grease at a sink in the corner of the shed. The luxury of a shower would have to wait till later. She still had her report to make out.

Her day's work recorded, she was hunting for some technical manuals along the shelves of the glass-enclosed office when a figure moved into the shed from outside. Something about the slope of those shoulders, the virile inflexibility of the sunburnt features, unearthed a raw little memory in her mind. 'Not you again,' she said as Todd Dillman strolled in through the open doorway. 'I thought you'd done all your viewing of the rare animal species this morning.'

'I came to take another look at the lesser known oil queen. Do you mind?'

The brilliance of evening streaming in through the shed frontage lit up his lazy smile. He had changed into a blue-flecked shirt and dark trousers. Patently ignoring him,

Rennie tossed a couple of technical magazines on to the desk from the shelf. He flicked his glance over them and said, harping back to that morning, 'So you finally got the bulldozer under way. There were moments when I had my doubts of you ever shifting it.'

'Earth-moving vehicles are not normally my responsibility.' She wished it didn't sound as though she were making excuses for herself. 'We have boys to attend to the mobile side of things. You probably wouldn't know it, but there's a world of difference between a mechanic and an engineer.'

'Between a mechanic and a *girl* engineer. Yes, I see what you mean.' His grin neatly reversed the barb. He made no effort to conceal the mocking contempt which had simmered below the surface of his smile at their first meeting.

Rennie dusted her hands. 'I've already gathered that female competition makes you nervous. So why the visit?' she asked.

'Curiosity, I guess.'

She was wondering, with no little confusion, how he had managed to get past the main gates. Security measures were strict and no one was allowed in or out of the diamond company limits without being given special clearance.

He was astute enough to read her mind, for he said with the same lazy grin, 'Coulton Kramer's an old friend of mine.'

Rennie bit back her annoyance. It had given her a certain superior feeling to keep him at a distance on the opposite side of the barbed wire this morning. Now here he was nosing his way around the office as though he owned it.

He ran a finger over a damaged drill component, then propped himself on the desk. 'First job?'

'Yes,' Rennie said shortly. Todd Dillman emanated a kind of latent vitality which made the place seem airless.

She could have pushed past him to the outdoors, but she was morally obliged to hang on until all the day's work chits had been handed in.

'I was about your age when I first came out to Africa. Kind of takes you by the throat, doesn't it? The raw scenery and the space.'

'I'll get used to it,' she replied, brushing the sticky hair from her temples as she tidied some bundles of cable.

Noticing the gesture, he pointed out, not without a trace of cheerful malice, 'This is only springtime. Wait until you feel the heat of the summer.'

'If you've survived, I'm sure I will.'

'I know, I know. Equality of the sexes and all that ...' Smiling, he rose to his considerable height, oozing his idle contempt.

The big Shangaan in charge of the diesel locomotives drove up and came to the pigeonhole window to thrust his time sheet through.

'Thank you, Zacharias. Goodnight.' Rennie lowered her head to give him a smile through the opening. He touched the battered trilby he always wore, but his grin went past her and she felt the man behind her acknowledge his nod of deference before he left to return to his truck.

She went to write up the notes in the records book. From where he leaned against a file Todd Dillman watched her, sizing up the sight of her in slim slacks and shirt as she moved. 'I don't get it,' he mused aloud, his green gaze blatantly appraising her. 'Neat figure ... small hands ... a tender look about the mouth ... You don't look to me the type who gets a kick out of swinging a hefty spanner.' And in his dry, belittling tones, 'Don't girls want to get married and settle down any more?'

In the drawer where she was placing the work sheet Rennie's hands had clenched tightly into fists. But she replied with an attempt at flippancy, 'If you mean don't we want to play the role of the little woman who stays conveniently tucked away in the background, the answer is no. Although we're well aware that the men would feel a whole lot safer if we were still wrapped up in the domesticities of home life waiting to pander to their needs.'

'As you say, times have changed.' His smile was loaded with amused scorn.

A group engaged on boreholing trudged up to hand in their sheets at the window. When they had departed Todd Dillman asked, 'What do you know about your employer?'

'Mr Kramer, the mine owner?' Rennie was mildly taken aback at this unexpected turn in the conversation. She pondered and said, 'I know he's something of a recluse and that few people have ever seen him. He was a geologist, I think, and he used to spend all his time prospecting.'

'Not the conventional prospecting,' Todd Dillman corrected her with grim humour.' He discovered his mine by the strictest application of scientific principles, by working with his head as well as his hands. It took him three years, during which time he almost starved, to mark out an area in the Northern Transvaal where he felt diamonds should logically be found. And here he found them. But it was a stubborn, lonely search. Blackwater fever and malaria almost killed him. Now he's no longer a strong man.' Another truck pulled up outside as Todd Dillman went on, 'Recently Coult had a set-back in health. He's a stubborn cuss. The mine hospital is pretty well equipped, but he needed special treatment. We had a fight to get him to go to Jo'burg.'

We? Did he mean him and Lila Harwood? As Rennie moved towards the pigeonhole window he rose from his lounging position to fill the office and concluded lazily, 'Coult will be away for a few weeks. That's why I thought I'd take a stroll down here this evening.'

Rennie nodded to the bearded Bantu in charge of the drilling section through the window opening. His mine helmet at a rakish angle he pushed his work sheet in and left, aiming his cheery salute past her to the man beside her in the office. 'Goodnight, baas.'

Rennie turned then. Something slowly dawning, she asked Todd Dillman, 'Are you telling me that you're here to keep an eye on things until Mr Kramer returns?'

'You could put it that way.' His green gaze flecked with steely irony challenged her lofty blue one. For a long moment while their glances remained locked in this way she was consumed by a resentment which unbalanced her to the point where she could have cheerfully hit him. Oh, she knew what he was thinking. He had been longing to spell it out for her ever since they had first met. No woman would ever be *his* equal. He was spelling it out for her now with his lazy, sardonic gleam.

The first to capitulate, though her blue eyes smouldered militantly, she swung away to lock the pigeonhole window. Then toning her emotions down to ice level she said with no more than a quiver in her voice, 'Well, I think you'll find that everything is in order. And now if you'll excuse me, I've had a long day.' She put the records book away in the drawer and picking up the engineering manuals she made for the door.

She was thrusting the key in the lock from the outside when Todd Dillman said, following her out, 'What I really came to tell you is that I'm organising a small reception at my house so that you can get to meet the mine personnel.'

Rennie looked at him, not knowing quite what to make of his remark. 'That isn't necessary,' she said coldly. 'The mine manager and his wife invited me to drinks at their house when I first arrived.'

'But that was a purely social occasion.' Was there the suggestion of playful malice about his smile? 'I'm talking about the men who have similar jobs to yourself at the mine—the excavation gang heads, the seasoned diggers and sluice operators. As you're on a level footing you should be formally introduced to our husky crew.'

Rennie dropped the keys to the office into her shirt pocket. Making for the outdoors, she said carefully, 'There's no need to go to all that trouble for me.'

'It's no trouble.' He accompanied her out of the shed into the fading evening light. 'Coult would expect me to lay on the official welcome for new staff. I thought Saturday afternoon would be a good time. You can't miss my house, it's the only one adjoining the airstrip.' He allowed his words to penetrate, then sized up her reluctance with a sadistic gleam. 'Afraid?'

'I'll be there.' Rennie lifted her chin where they had stopped on the road and faced him squarely.

'Two o'clock okay?'

'If you say so.'

Indolently sure of himself, he viewed her at close quarters under a sky shot with saffron flame and drawled, 'How are you making out with your buddy at the mine face, the chief engineer?'

'We get along,' she replied primly. 'Leith is a craftsman. He knows his job. I'm looking forward to learning all I can from him.'

Todd Dillman grinned narrowly. 'You're a rotten liar, Rennie what's-your-name. Bonell is a loafer and he'll leave you to do all the hard graft whenever he gets the opportunity.'

His insufferable bumptiousness again! 'Are you trying to frighten me off before I start?' she purred icily.

'I couldn't do that, could I?' His mocking look was all-encompassing. 'We both know that tough engineers have no nerves.'

Reversing the subtleties, she tilted an eyebrow at him and purred back, 'Could it be that you're envious?'

His grin in no way impaired, he took his leave of her then and her breath fluttered like a caged bird in her throat as she turned thankfully away. Of all the conceited, egoistical *men* she had ever had to tangle with he was the

worst! He was one of those detestable types who still wore
his male superiority like a badge. Well, he was welcome to
it! And if he thought that standing in for the diamond
mine owner gave him some sort of edge over her he was
welcome to that too!

As she strutted along the road home a couple of minutes
later a station wagon, all quiet varnished wood magnifi-
cence, whispered over the dusty surface alongside. Todd
Dillman waved a hand chummily through the open window
as he went by.

CHAPTER TWO

ON a bench of kimberlite rock the dynamite holes had been
delicately sealed. The urgent note of the hooter warned
everyone to take cover and men scuttled from the scene.
With the detonator poised a hush fell over the area devoid
of life, then the whole kimberlite face split heavenwards,
blackening the sky with rocky fragments. The noise and the
dust receded. The electric shovels moved in. It was just
another day at the Kramer diamond mine.

Rennie dusted herself off beside a four-wheeled scraper
and trudged to retrieve her rucksack. She had doused her
temples with cool water from her flask and was slaking the
grittiness from her throat when a young man approached
from the direction of the main work site. 'Are you the girl
they call Rennie? The assistant to the chief engineer?' He
was about her own age, of slender build with thin sensitive features and a kind of eager, worried look.

'That's me.' Rennie touched her peaked cap in greeting.

'I'm Darrell Timpson,' he smiled shyly. 'I've got to go
into Wykveld to pick up a rail consignment of trommel
and jig spares. But as I haven't a clue what a trommel or a

jig looks like I'll need some assistance to vet the things. Can you spare the time to help a chap out?'

'What, go into town now?'

'It's all right,' he assured her hurriedly. 'I've checked with the powers that be.'

Rennie couldn't believe her luck. A chance to get away for a while! She said with a thoughtful expression, 'We'll need a truck for the spares. Mine's not exactly air-cushioned comfort.'

The young man replied with the glimmer of a grin, 'I'm game if you are.'

Was she! A thirty-mile drive and a chance to take a peep at the African stores. 'Let's go!' she said with a laugh.

He fell into step beside her and as they rounded the rubble of blasted rock he queried eagerly, 'You're from England, aren't you?'

She smiled, 'That's right.'

'My home's in Canterbury, Kent.' There was a tremor of pride in his voice.

'Kent, England?' Surprise and pleasure mingled in her gaze. She gave a disbelieving laugh. 'And I thought I was the only greenhorn within miles of this place.' Then quickly, 'I'm sorry. I didn't mean that you were——'

'That's all right,' he drooped a pale grin. 'I've been here two months, but I know I still stick out like a sore finger.'

'I haven't seen you around the quarrying area?' She guided him to where her truck stood, little more than a dusty heap beside the site office.

'I came out as a trainee grid fitter.' He held the door as she climbed in. 'But I suppose I didn't show much promise. At the moment I'm doing odd jobs around maintenance and the administration block.'

Rennie started the engine and the whole tiny cabin where they sat began to shake and rattle as though it were stricken with the ague. She looked at him with a twinkle. 'You see what I mean?'

He stretched his legs in the clatter and twinkled back, not without a note of fight in his voice, 'This is the land of adventure, isn't it?'

'Right! Road, here we come!' Her hair wisping out from her cap, her boots caked with earth, Rennie put the engine into motion feeling lighter than she had done for a week.

They jolted over the rugged landscape towards the residential compound and the main gates. There was a ten-minute hold-up while they were checked and allowed to drive out, then the bonnet of the truck adding a musical rattle they set off for town. With the barbed wire falling behind and the countryside opening up in front of them the day developed a sparkle. Due no doubt to the sneaking feeling of freedom experienced by both, the atmosphere inside the cab was companionable with only the barest trace of shyness.

The road from the mine was dusty and arid, but soon they were skirting the slopes of the settlement with their neat bungalows and valiant spread of green in the patchwork gardens. At the roadside the Vukasi general store displaying fruit and farm produce had become an established meeting place for the nearby villagers. The women wore brightly coloured sarongs and their necks, arms and legs winked with a profusion of brass adornments, bead necklaces and bangles. The piccaninnies were as gay and boisterous as children anywhere. When they spotted the truck a flurry of pink palms and wide smiles hailed the young man with the dark red hair seated in the cab. Rennie commented as they went by, 'You appear to have made a hit with the locals.'

He shrugged modestly. 'I've been doing some sketching in my spare time. The kids and mothers will sit for hours for a copper or two.' He hastened to add self-consciously, 'It's only a hobby. I don't shine at anything particularly.'

He was suffering from an acute case of dwindling self-confidence, or lack of it, to be more exact, Rennie decided. She said above her private thoughts, 'I envy anyone who has the talent for capturing the colour of Africa. There's so much of it about it hurts the eyes.'

'I prefer to work with charcoal,' Darrell put in diffidently. 'These people have a shape and grace which is quite something. On canvas one would have to tone down one's choice of shades or the whole thing would become a daub.' He added meditatively, 'I saw some watercolours in Johannesburg once. The wash of land and sky softened the effect no end. I thought they were just right.'

Was that a clue to his personality? Rennie wondered. Insipid, she would have called those watercolours. She liked the wild, strong colours of the red earth and the hot blue sky, of the jungle green in drying river beds and the stunning and attractive contrast of gay prints against polished ebony skins.

The route skirted the remnants of a rocky stream, the source of the local water supply, and on a bend they passed a farm strip used for growing food for the mine where fat cabbages squatted in rows like obscene, overblown roses. The air wafting in through the open windows of the cab was pungent and dusty, but neither occupant gave a thought to this minor inconvenience. Rennie felt comfortable in cotton shirt and brace dungarees.

Darrell, still in thoughtful mood, eyed the changing scenery and licking the beads of sweat from his upper lip mused, 'It's funny to think that here we're just approaching summer, whereas where we come from it's the other way round. At night time I try and picture dusk over the Kent countryside now. The trees will be just turning from brown to gold, and there might be the cry of an owl over the fields.'

'Homesick?' Rennie spared him a sympathetic glance from her place at the wheel. It stirred him out of his reverie and as though it was a lapse he couldn't afford he replied staunchly, 'No. I came to settle out here. It's only a question of getting used to the idea.'

She sensed an inner battle going on behind those drawn, sensitive features and felt too uncertain to make any comment. Besides, her attention had roamed beyond him to the view on his side of the road. They were passing the Harwood house with its tall gates and high walls. One could see no more than the gabled roof and a little of the pillared stoep, but the whole place was steeped in an aura of wealth and remoteness. What was going on behind those walls no one could say, and Rennie told herself that she wasn't in the least bit interested.

The truck clattered by, its steering not all that steady on the rough dirt road. Opening up in front of them was the route across the rolling veld. To right and left the low distant ridges of mountains were a dim, misty lilac against the hazy blue of the sky. Close at hand orange bluffs vied with the metallic sweep of coarse grasses and here and there, watered by winter rains, was the green of flat-topped acacias, the feathery yellow blossom of the cassia and the silvery foliage of terminalia trees.

With the wide open spaces one's sense of freedom expanded. Darrell put his feet up on an old petrol can beneath the dashboard and remarked comfortably, 'At this rate it'll take us about an hour to get there.'

'And the same back,' Rennie said in a similar mischievous vein. She had made a couple of trips to town in her own time, but there was something distinctly pleasurable about bouncing along an uncluttered road during working hours.

The journey was not without its ups and downs. They got stuck in a spruit, one of those rocky watercourses which took one by surprise round the sloping bends, and near a scattering of native huts they were obliged to ask for water for the panting radiator—it had occurred to neither to fill up while they were coaxing the truck through the spruit—

but they arrived in Wykveld in good spirits and none the worse for the trip.

Rennie made straight for the railway goods yard. From Darrell's list she checked over the consignment of machine parts, then while they were being loaded they strolled into town. It was really only a business centre for the northern outposts of the Transvaal, but it possessed a very attractive main street with colourful stores befitting an African community and a hotel with a pretty bougainvillea-clad entrance.

It was here that the pair, dusty and thirsty, finally ended up. 'I'll have a cold beer. What about you?'

'The same,' Rennie responded cheerfully as her companion led the way inside. In a cool lounge they found a table facing the breeze and for the next ten minutes the pitchers of thirst-quenching liquid claimed all their attention.

Darrell was the first to finish. He clapped his mug down on the table and said grandiloquently, 'What about another?'

Rennie looked at his lobster-pink face and at her half-depleted contents. 'Not for me. One drink is enough at this time of day,' she replied.

He laughed harshly and rose. 'The Afrikaaners throw this stuff back like water.' As he went to re-order Rennie sat not knowing quite what to make of her young workmate. He seemed to alternate between moods of manly bravado and youthful despair.

He returned and was soon making short work of his second draught of beer. Rennie finished her own and they were leisurely soaking up the scene when he drew her attention in from the garden with a low, smiling exclamation. 'Well, look who's over there! Our locum boss and his lady.'

The place was fairly empty at this time of day, but in the thin drift of people out in the lobby, Rennie saw Todd Dillman with his hand on Lila's elbow. She didn't know whether it was her companion's familiar reference to the pair making her feel glaringly new to the life out here, or the sight of Todd Dillman, striking in a casual way in silk shirt and fawn slacks and every inch the suave escort, or a combination of both, which filled her with irritation.

She rose and said abruptly, 'It's time we were going, Darrell.'

He looked up at her in surprise. 'What for? We're entitled to a break before we make the trip back.'

'I know,' she reasoned, 'but we've got to walk through town to pick up the truck and it's a long drive to the mine.'

'I suppose you're right.' Reluctantly he got to his feet and they drifted out of the side entrance.

There had been no one else in the lounge, so Rennie didn't know whether they had been seen leaving or not. Not that it mattered. They were doing a job and there was no restriction on their time until they got back to the Vukasi mine.

On the return journey it appeared that the drink had loosened Darrell's tongue. Either that or the last traces of his shyness had vanished during the hour or so they had been together, for he chatted easily about their surroundings. 'If we had the time we could drive out beyond the sandstone bluffs. In the normal course of events you could travel the length of this road a dozen times a day and never see a wild animal, but out there on the plains there's buffalo and lion and the usual wildebeest and stuff. During the rains wildlife is pretty scarce, but in the dry season they roam for miles in search of water, even from as far as the Kruger national park, which is quite a way when you consider the rough terrain in between.'

Rennie coaxed the truck over a low stone bridge and commented, 'You seem to know a lot about Africa.'

'It's in my veins. Or at least I'm told it is.' He wore that enigmatic, slightly bitter smile which puzzled her and with a half laugh she said,

'But I don't understand. I thought you said you were new to the country?'

'Never set foot in it in my life until a couple of months ago.' He was gazing out at the rugged landscape as he spoke and from there he went on in enlightening tones, 'A couple of generations ago my family were settlers out here. Every one of them made good in farming and mining and the white hunter business, but the male line died out and with only the women left they decided to pack up and go back to England. I'm the only offshoot from those days and for as long as I can remember I've had maiden aunts and sisters and my mother singing the praises of the country. My grandmother grubbed a tobacco farm out of arid land with her bare hands out here. She's eighty-three, but she would come back tomorrow if my grandfather were alive.'

Rennie digested this information and the weighty way it was delivered. She said after a lengthy pause, 'For a young man South Africa is still the land of opportunity.'

'It depends what one is looking for,' he shrugged, then went back to dreaming over the scenery. 'When I was at school I had a mate who was mad on boats. Not the ocean-going kind—river cruisers. He got this thing about starting up in business on the Norfolk Broads. Together we worked out a fairly profitable scheme for hiring out river craft and running boating holidays.'

'What happened?' Rennie asked.

'As far as I know Bob's going ahead with his plans.'

First it was 'we', then it was 'Bob'. Rennie kept her gaze out front. Poor Darrell! He was torn between upholding the family tradition and making a name for himself in the land of their choice, and following his own instincts for a happy existence. Unfortunately it was his own problem and he would have to work it out for himself. Yet she couldn't help feeling a niggling impatience at his irresolute attitude. Surely there was some excitement to be derived out of living and working in a country so extravagantly life-filled

and fabulous. And why didn't he make up his mind to give
it a fair chance for a year or so instead of dithering with no
real set course either way!

They were on the flat stretch of road with the panorama
of distant mountains, thorny bushveld and coppery green
grass all around them. Rennie was idling with her own
thoughts at the wheel when, from a pool of shade, two
darker shapes moved not far from the road. They went
nervously, stopping to look and listen at the approach of
the truck. 'Duikers,' Darrell said. 'One of the smaller
antelopes.'

'They're darlings,' Rennie laughed softly, 'but terrified
of us.'

'They're a bit off the beaten track, but most of the wildlife has grown accustomed to cars. Slow down,' Darrell
suggested. 'We might get a closer look.'

Rennie complied, though it was a bit too much to expect
the shy duiker to remain on show, and sure enough with
the wheeze and shudder of the engine they became no
more than fawn flashes weaving through the undergrowth.
The truck was merrily slewing to right and left over the
road following their antics when the loud, imperious blast
of a horn came to the pair inside the cab. A window in the
back framed their young heads and shoulders and jointly
they turned to see what all the commotion was about.
Rennie said indignantly, eyeing the distant glinting shape,
'There's nothing like wanting all the road, is there? They're
miles behind us yet.' Though she had only seen it once
before she recognised the shape and colour of that strident
machine.

Apparently Darrell too had gathered who was behind
them, for he advised with a tolerant grin, 'Better pull over
and let the royalty pass.'

'Easier said than done,' Rennie grimaced, battling with
the faulty steering. 'This thing's all right for bouncing
around the mine site, but it doesn't take too kindly to main-

taining a straight course.' She didn't want to say so, but she had partly lost control of it in following the duikers' movements and as though it was an unruly pony it was some time before she could coax it over to the grass verge. As she did so Todd Dillman's station wagon shot by and with a long wail of the horn sounding in their ears—as a broad hint, no doubt, Rennie clenched her teeth—it disappeared to become a small speck in the distance ahead. She glowered after it in disgust. 'I thought we'd left all the roadhogs behind in Britain.'

'That's the normal speed around here,' Darrell excused the man, to her further annoyance. 'The distances are so vast everything would come to a standstill if they did a meagre forty or fifty.'

'It's only thirty miles to Vukasi,' she scoffed. 'But I suppose he had to let us know he was around. He's that type.'

She had noticed the head of spun copper next to his in the front seat, but it was Darrell who referred to his female companion. 'Lila's crazy for speed. Perhaps he was burning up the tyres to please her.'

Rennie couldn't imagine Todd Dillman doing anything unless it pleased himself. She said begrudgingly, 'I've noticed that she's a superb horsewoman.'

'Superb everything,' came the light reply. 'She flies her own private plane and drives a racing sports which can beat anything on the road. She's got everything she wants except Todd. I gather he's a man who likes to make up his own mind, but the pressure must be wearing him down. Lila's quite a dish.'

One couldn't take offence at Darrell's chat. There was no rancour or envy or malice in his tones—Rennie was beginning to suspect he was incapable of these full-blooded emotions—but something in the free and easy way he discussed the affairs of the two who had just shot by rasped on her nerves. She said coolly, 'You're not short on local gossip, are you?'

'In a small community like ours, stuck out in the middle of nowhere, you soon get to know what's going on,' he replied, blithely oblivious to her condemning tones. 'You'd be amazed at the intrigue that goes on under cover of digging diamonds out of the ground.'

'I bet I would.' Rennie swung the wheel over the last lap of their journey.

'Half the wives of the mine personnel haven't got enough to do. They spend their time organising posh afternoon teas and dinner parties. Chaps like me are welcome anywhere,' he said, to give him his due, self-effacingly. 'And as you might guess, bachelors of Todd Dillman's status are in high demand at these functions. Leith Bonell's another one who so far has managed to avoid the ties of matrimony, but Leith has an eye for the dusky ladies. Then there's Johann Wenhold from the ore-washing plant. He brought his new wife back from Durban and it turns out she was the old flame of Otto Lange in the block caving team. As you can imagine, the air's like dynamite between them. And I could tell you about Doctor Dunbar at the mine hospital. Nobody knows for sure, but——'

'I think that's enough to be going on with,' Rennie cut in firmly with a wry look. 'In any case, I don't intend to become involved in what goes on in the mining community. I've got a job to do and I shall keep personal relationships out of it.'

'That's what they all say,' Darrell shrugged with a knowing smile, 'but they all end up suffering the slings and arrows, as old man Shakespeare put it.'

Rennie eyed him stringently. 'I don't see any scars on you,' she said pointedly. 'And you're not new to Vukasi.'

'I suppose that's because I've always been a bit of a square peg.'

Did he mean that his inability to adapt to mining life

gave him an immunity from its emotional entanglements? Rennie considered his reply. If so, she had no need to worry. Wasn't she here a little against her own will also?

They were approaching the settlement and still in informative mood Darrell pointed out the Dutch-style residence at the side of the road. 'That's Lila's pad. Her old man's a gold-mining magnate in Johannesburg. He bought the house, which used to be a museum, as a retreat from the pressures of the city, but piling up gold must be an absorbing pastime. He rarely visits the place. It was Lila who talked her father into engaging Todd Dillman to re-design the grounds. A smart move when you come to think of it. She has him all to herself whenever she comes to visit.'

Rennie was glad that they were nearing the end of the trip. To her mind the conversation was getting into an annoying rut.

CHAPTER THREE

THEY rattled past the store and through a wooded stretch where weaver birds and blue-black starlings fluttered among the branches. Further on the barbed wire of the mine compound came into view. At the main gates they were seen through by burly Ted Mills of Security.

From there Rennie drove Darrell straight to the maintenance sheds. He stood about while the boys were unloading the crates wearing that strained look and air of the misfit now that they were back at the mine. 'Thanks for the ride. It made a change from work,' he joked feebly up at the cab. 'I suppose you've gathered I don't go a bundle on the diamond business.'

Looking down at him from where she sat, Rennie saw a vulnerability in his thin, boyish features which made her feel ashamed of her impatience earlier. He reminded her of a dutiful youth trying hard to shine on the sports field when he didn't really like football at all.

'You're not sure if it's really you?' she clarified with a smile. Her gaze fathomed something of the way he felt and sincerity was in her tones as she told him, 'I do know what you mean, Darrell. More than you think.'

A rap on the truck indicated that the crates were clear and as she started up he gave her a wave. 'See you around.'

''Bye!' She watched him trudge off into the shed. Bouncing over the rough terrain towards the quarrying site, she was struck by the fact that he had made no attempt to further their friendship. And come to think of it, he hadn't asked her a thing about herself. The only thing that Darrell was concerned with was his own impermanency. But he was all right, she smiled reflectively. At least he hadn't treated her as though she had two heads or something because she was an engineer.

It was later when she was reminded of the other incident which had taken place on the drive back from Wykveld.

It had been a busy afternoon. She was called out to a vacuumatic machine used for bedrock cleaning which was functioning erratically and a mobile stacker conveyor had got jammed while discarding sand in a worked-out area. She had walked the half mile or so there and back over excavated rocky ground and was taking a break with a mug of coffee when an unbelievable sight met her eyes. Quickly she clapped her mug down and went to where Spike Tshabala from the vehicles unit was preparing to tow her mine truck away. 'Where are you going with my transport?' she asked crossly.

Spike blinked at her from where he was linking up the grappling hook. 'Baas Dillman told me to take it up to the field depot.'

'I suppose he knows it's a three-mile walk back to the residential compound?' she tapped her foot.

'I got orders to supply you with a new range truck.' The old man's features were puckered with suppressed humour and knowing that she had been the subject of their conversation she asked tartly, eyeing him closely, 'And what else did boss Dillman say?'

Spike's chuckles burst from his throat, high-pitched and musical. 'He say, just like all women you're a menace on the road.' He climbed into his pick-up, shaking in his plump, bent way, enjoying the joke hugely.

'Did he indeed! Well, that was just typical of *him*.' Rennie watched the pick-up move off, knowing much more than Spike did that there was a wealth of meaning in that comment.

There was no time to dwell on it, however, for shortly afterwards Johann Wenhold came slewing up to the site office and tumbling out of his conveyance with an agitated look, 'Is the chief here?'

'Leith?' Rennie shook her head. 'I thought he was with you at the field screening plant.'

'He was, but there's no sign of him now.'

Johann's frustration was obvious, so she asked, 'What's wrong?'

'Can't stop to go into it now. Better come and see for yourself.' He waved her to his truck.

Now what? Rennie thought wearily as they bounced over the uneven ground to the tall building in the distance. Once indoors Johann took her straight to the trouble. The vibrating screen taking the concentrates from the primary and secondary washing pans was working at a crazy tilt. She could see at a glance the cause of his worry. Precious diamondiferous sludge was being directed towards the waste pipes from where it could take days, possibly weeks, to re-screen.

There was no time to be lost. 'I'll attend to it,' she told Johann, dutifully opening her tool box. But later, after she had wrestled with a problem far beyond her comprehension, she told herself that one day she was going to stand in for Leith and take on something too big to handle, and then they would all be in trouble.

Saturday came. A day flooded with sunshine and the sharp, sweet scent of the blossoming acacias. The mining area lay in shimmering stillness in the distance, but the residential compound was in gay holiday mood with workers strolling in brilliantly patterned shirts and smart cotton suits and the trees and flower gardens lining the shopping centre contrasting colourfully with the aridness of the veld.

Basket in hand, Rennie strolled round the greengrocery and the bakery stores revelling in the thought of the whole weekend before her. She bought crisp rolls and dew-fresh lettuce and salad items from the farm and stopped off to watch a game on the bowling green on her way back to her bungalow.

After lunch she showered and put on a pair of washed-out denims, which despite their frayed state hugged her slim hips attractively, and a much-laundered tee-shirt with a faded horseshoe design. Before the mirror she paused with the usual problem, that dark glistening cloud tumbling to her shoulders. Her eyes on her reflection, she ran a brush through the long tresses and lingered perversely over the task. Not even for her father would she sacrifice her hair.

Placing the brush down at last, she found a soft white cap with a neb at the front. The dark mass she coiled up and hid away beneath it. But what she saw in the mirror drew a frustrated sigh from her. What did it leave? Full velvet-soft lips, the lower one of which drooped prettily when she smiled to show girlish white teeth, thick-lashed blue eyes, pale around the irises, deep violet at the edges, and a gaze forthright yet innocent.

She swung away. Well, who cared? It was a gorgeous day and she intended to make the most of it.

The airstrip lay on a flat stretch behind the Vukasi general store, no more than a pleasant walk away.

Once outside the main gates of the mine Rennie strolled enjoying the freedom and peace of the countryside. Along the track below the hill settlement where the top executives of the mining company were permitted to live outside the compound, there was a tangle of lush greenery beside the road and the soothing sound of running water from the nearby streams.

She passed a village family, the mother padding along gracefully in bare feet, a loaded basket on her head, the children skipping over the dusty, ochre-coloured surface. And through the trees she caught glimpses of the straw huts of Vukasi huddled in tiers beside the mustard-coloured Zamba river.

A short track hacked out of the undergrowth led her out to the airstrip. The rush of cool air was welcome, the sight a little breathtaking after the enclosed feeling of the mine road. Beyond the concrete strip the flat, open country-side was a mass of spring flowers, a red and yellow carpet which stretched as far as the eye could see until it was lost in the purple-grey shadows of distant hills. A hush hung over the scene and it was easy to imagine the land as it once was before the voortrekkers came and made it their own.

Todd Dillman's house backed on to the greenery of the river. Framed against leadwood and cassia trees, it stood in splendid isolation facing the incredible view. It had a green corrugated roof and cream walls and a large, smooth lawn scalloping out under ornamental trees and shrubbery.

It was just two when Rennie arrived. On the steps she saw a group of beefy-looking individuals making their way indoors. Todd Dillman was there in a lightweight pale blue suit and dark blue open-necked shirt.

'Good afternoon. Spot on time.' His mocking gaze roved over her youthful curves. 'Your engineer's training, I bet.'

'Were you expecting me to turn up half an hour late in true feminine style?' she asked smoothly.

He replied in the same vein, 'I knew you'd make it. You're too gone on this equality thing to let that happen.' And then with something a little menacing about his smile he guided her towards the door. 'Come inside and meet your friends.'

Over the threshold Rennie was met by the powerful masculine odour of sweating bodies, cigarette smoke, strong drink and pungent hair oil. In the taproom atmosphere Todd stuck a brimming tankard of beer into her hand. 'Here, this should do for a start.' And propelling her before him, 'Come on, I'll introduce you around.'

They stopped beside a burly figure with pugilistic features whom she had seen supervising the workers at the slimes dam. 'This is Len Koornof. Len, meet your partner in crime at the mine, our new second engineer.' Her hand was taken in a brawny grip and she smiled at the unintelligible Afrikaans greeting.

'And this is Kobie Dykman who keeps an eye on the tailings dump.' She was turned towards a thick-set monkey-faced man with black stubble on his chin and a squashed cheroot in his mouth. 'How's it going, Kobe? A buddy of yours here, our new engineer. Rennie's the name . . .'

One by one she got to know every man in the room. Soon her hand became a throbbing limp thing. In between swigging their drinks the miners were friendly and eager to help, and Todd looked on with a whimsical glint as each one noisily offered his advice.

She drank her own beer to be matey, but her attention was mainly taken up with the decor of the room. It was totally unexpected. The walls were of palest lilac, the curtains and upholstery the fraction of a shade darker. There was a glass-topped table holding some polished pieces of rock crystal, two columns of sculptured glass and a single white waxen flower. Another circular marble-topped table catching the light of the windows held an arrangement of white, cream, and ivory porcelain and a bunch of Shasta daisies in a plain white vase. The overall effect was cool and restful.

But it was lost on the crowd who were raising the roof with their loud guffaws. Rennie winced as unsteady hands slopped drink on to the cream carpet and caught Todd eyeing her with amused interest. 'It's washable,' he remarked drily.

After that she shut her mind to the awful sight of burning cigarettes resting on impeccable surfaces and dusty boots propped on downy cushions and tried to appear indifferent.

Leith Bonell was the life and soul of the party. Always boisterous when he had a drink, he came and dropped a big arm around her shoulders. 'Great to have you with us, kid,' he raised his glass. And crunched as she was against him, he asked, 'What do you think about the stuff they're sending us these days, Todd? Reckon she'll make a chief engineer one day?'

'I wouldn't be at all surprised,' Todd replied ironically.

Rennie was beginning to feel bruised in that ape-like embrace, but she made a point of smiling up at the unlovely face and commenting nicely, 'There's only one chief around here, and that's you, Leith. I'll need years of practice to be as good as you.'

Swelling to twice his size at the praise, the chief hugged her and guffawed, 'You play your cards right and I'll see what I can do.'

Far from wishing to put an end to the embrace, Rennie was finding her feet at last in the situation which Todd had plunged her into. Though he looked on with a smile and drew negligently on his cigarette as she clowned with Leith she felt that she had got under his skin in some way by buttering up the chief and she found a peculiar enjoyment in laying it on with a trowel. 'Out of all the men at the mine,

I think your job is the most exacting,' she told him admiringly. And measuring his barrel chest with her gaze, 'But luckily you've got tremendous stamina. Only a tough type like you could handle it.'

'Hell, but you're right!' Leith looked dazed at his own omnipotence. He threw his drink back, wiped his mouth on the back of his hand and voiced a sudden brainwave. 'Hey, me and some of the boys are going to work out a motor-bike circuit near the tailings dump tomorrow. Why don't you come over and watch us do a hundred over the dunes? How about it, Todd?'

'Count me out,' he shook his head. 'I'll be fully occupied tomorrow.'

What he meant was he would be spending the day with Lila. Rennie lowered her lashes swiftly at the thought. A short time ago she hadn't even known that Todd or Lila existed. Now she found herself constantly running up against them, linking them in her mind as though they were part and parcel of her existence.

Letting none of this show, however, she smiled prettily and replied, 'Well, of course I'll come and watch you, Leith.'

Pleasure was written all over his face as he looked around for something to replenish his glass with and in doing so brought forth with uninhibited contentment a stomach-rumbling burp. Rennie caught the full force of his sour breath. She was careful not to let her smile slip, however, knowing that Todd's sardonic gleam was glued on her.

He said before drifting lazily away, 'I can see our new recruit is feeling at home in your company, chief. Keep up the good work and I'll go and rustle up some more drinks.'

Rennie knew that he watched her from a distance after that so she stayed with Leith, larking and laughing for the best part of the afternoon. With the chief's robust good humour fermented into almost high spirits by the drink it wasn't difficult to keep up the jollity, especially when occasionally some of the other men joined in. It was only when a pair of dice was produced and the miners gathered into a noisy group to discuss gambling techniques that she was able to disappear through the adjoining door to catch her breath.

The peace of the room she found herself in washed over her, soothing her throbbing temples. Gradually as her calm returned she began to take in her surroundings. She had never seen a house like it, but the effect was similar to that of sitting within the sound of a cool playing fountain or walking on a lonely cliff top with the wind in one's face.

In window-lit spaces bowls of dried grasses, teasels and seed heads gave a creamy gold warmth to the pale walls and furnishings. Jade animal figures on perspex bases stood translucently serene, and on a snakeskin-covered table a stoneware bowl held a miniature cypress forest with rocks and moss to give the impression of a natural rugged landscape.

As far as she could see into the other rooms beyond there was something which unobtrusively beckoned the eye. A group of porcelain birds on white shelves, a pastoral bunch of wild herbs in a salt glaze jug, pink quartz elephants. But not all the colours were subdued. Curiosity got the better of her and she moved on into a room across a hallway.

She was studying the daring effect of a poppy red sofa against geranium pink walls when Todd said behind her, 'For a moment I thought you were comparing the pretty colour schemes, but engineers don't go in for that kind of thing, do they?'

'Of course not,' she replied, riveting her gaze beyond the window. 'I was simply admiring the view.'

'I practise interior decorating in my spare time. Most of this stuff I had sent up from the stores in Jo'burg. The personal bits and pieces have been with me for a long time.' Sure of himself, he came to stand beside her, but ignoring the outdoors he went on with a drawl, 'You must have been struck by it in some way or you wouldn't have got this far. Care to offer an opinion?'

Who could deny that the rooms were exquisitely balanced, yet Rennie said evasively as she turned, 'It seems a lot of trouble to go to for a short stay.'

'That's not wishful thinking, I hope?' He eyed her with a wicked gleam, and in a relaxed pose he told her, 'There's nothing short about my occupation. It could take ten years to re-design the grounds of Rosedale. Working with nature is a slow process. An elderly colleague of mine in Krugersdorp has been landscaping a property there for almost twenty years.'

So Lila knew what she was about when she got her father to engage Todd for the job of streamlining Rosedale. Rennie trained her glance on a bowl of scarlet and mauve anemones across the room. Her pulses behaving erratically, she was acutely aware of the man beside her, yet a curious reluctance to break away from him made her say blandly, 'I can't imagine anyone living out in the wilds like this unless they have to. But then you've got your entertainment laid on. All Africa at your doorstep,' she nodded to the rolling vista beyond the window, 'and unlimited privileges in a mining community where a bachelor is the rarest animal.'

'You've been listening to Timpson's gossip.' His grin didn't deny the implication, something which irritated her more than she cared to admit. He thrust his hands into his pockets and viewed her idly. 'I suppose he's told you the whole sorry story of his life by now, and how he hates it out here?'

'Darrell is homesick and uncertain of his future. But you couldn't understand that, could you? You've always known what you want and how to get it.' Itching as she was to take a stab at his male conceit, she found herself confronting him a little recklessly.

He smiled with not one chink in his self-assurance. 'The Transvaal breeds 'em tough—I learned that a long time ago.

Timpson lacks backbone and without it the life he's trying to lead will make mincemeat of him.'

'I don't agree.' She raised her chin. 'I believe, given the right kind of encouragement, he could grow to like it out here, and become strong and accomplished.'

'Like Bonell?' Sarcasm in his tones, Todd's smile was crooked. Was there a crack in his self-assurance after all?

'Leith is a man doing a man's job.' Rennie was quick to take advantage of a little gained ground.

'Sure he is, with about as much finesse as a ham-handed ape, but I gather he's the type you'd like to model yourself on, muscling in on the act as you are.'

'I could hardly model myself on a landscape gardener, could I?' she replied sweetly. 'A man who spends all his time with flowers and trees.' She wished he had been slight and weedy-looking so that her taunt would make itself felt, but he wasn't. He was all width and lean-hipped and his green eyes glinted with metallic humour in the hard planes of his face.

'Some day I'll take you on a tour of the Rosedale grounds,' he said with the suggestion of a threat in his voice. 'You might be surprised at what you see.'

'Wouldn't Lila object?' Though she put the query lightly Rennie had no idea what possessed her to speak so boldly.

'Why should she? A mining engineer doesn't offer any direct competition.' Unmoved, Todd's ironic glance was all-embracing.

'Could anyone compete with the gold bricks in her father's bank?' She was goaded into meeting his gaze with a look of her own.

He gave her a deprecating smile. 'Money apart, Lila doesn't try to be anything but what she is, a woman.'

'But something of a superwoman the way she rides a horse,' Rennie intoned. 'And from what I hear she's fairly gadget-minded—racing cars, and flying aeroplanes. In fact she seems to do it all so much better than a man.'

'If she saw you now she'd swear that was a gleam of professional jealousy in your eye.'

He looked aggravatingly at ease, and Rennie was searching for another salvo when an uproar from the other room reminded her that they were not alone in the house. And feeling that the ground was becoming more and more like quicksand beneath her feet she said, turning to go, 'I ought to be getting back to the others. I only really came out for a second.'

Todd took her arm and guiding her out he spoke drily. 'Bonell will be wondering what kept you.'

Thoroughly soused by this time, the mining crews were testing their lungs with old South African ditties when Rennie rejoined them. She sat on the sofa wedged in tightly on either side, trying to pick up the words as everyone sang gustily, while Leith stood waving a cheese straw baton hopelessly out of time, and the rest of the revellers waltzed giddily in pairs round the room.

She didn't see Todd again until they had all graduated out on to the lawn and after a few turns of a very shaky conga decided to call it a day. With the lusty gathering breaking up she was turning away thankfully—though she hoped it didn't show—towards home when he appeared beside her on the path. 'Some initiation party!' He lifted an eyebrow with wry humour.

'Too bad you're not an engineer, you could have joined in,' she smiled.

'I was meant for gracious living,' he shrugged with a gleam, then nodded to his car. 'I'll give you a lift back.'

Rennie stiffened. 'I enjoy walking. It's only a short distance.'

'It's all right. I've got to go to the mine compound.'

Persuasive or forceful, she didn't know which, but she ended up sitting beside him and being transported along the riverside road where the afternoon sun flashed intermittently through the overhead greenery showering coins of copper light on the dusty surface below.

Her nerves had tightened up again. She felt physically spent. Not so much from her activities at the drinking party but from pitting herself against the powerful personality of the man seated beside her. She couldn't wait to get back to the safety of her own quarters.

There was no hold-up at the main gates. Todd was waved through and he made straight for the residential compound. As he drove along the wide avenues separating the neat habitations he asked, 'Which one is yours?'

'Number ninety-seven. The end one on E block,' she told him woodenly.

'The bachelor section?'

She let him have his little joke.

Though the flat stretch close to the mine was semi-desert, the gardens of the bungalows had been carefully nurtured and all kinds of blossom and greenery trailed over the fences. Every so often a block had been specially planted with shrubs and trees and on the open flank of the compound facing the sweeping plains a line of hardy thorn trees gave shelter from searing high veld winds.

It was here that Rennie's bungalow made a bleak outpost, the last one on a slight rise overlooking a sea of sun-dried savannah. Todd pulled up at the kerb and she got out with a cool, 'Thank you for the ride,' hoping that he would turn away again and drive off. But he climbed out and followed her up the path to the door. She opened it, giving no indication that she knew he was there, and went inside. He was right behind her, indolently inspecting the bare rooms with their plain wooden furniture, the small kitchen and the enamel mugs and plates.

As a large hint she went outside again and on the steps she tapped her foot. 'Do you mind? I've got things to do.'

'You're not going to sit with your knitting!' He drifted out sardonically.

'I have some letters to write,' she lied.

Todd stood on the step beside her. She felt that he was taking in the pathetic patch of lawn and bare soil beds. Her gaze was on them too so that she was taken completely off her guard when in one neat movement he reached out and flicked off her cap.

As her hair came tumbling down about her shoulders she asked angrily, 'Now why did you do that?'

He had moved down a step. With his mocking green glance on a level with her smouldering blue one he said thoughtfully, 'I'm just wondering what makes a girl like you tick. You could have had a chintzy house with a pretty garden like the wives of the mine personnel go for, but you chose the hermit way of life. There isn't a flower or a powder puff in sight.' He eyed the effect of her dark tresses, the curls and tips of which were bronzed by the lowering sun, and with his head on one side mused, 'You could have your hair cropped like mine, but that might be taking things too far?' With a quizzical gleam he tossed her cap at her and giving her a brief salute, 'So long, Rennie the engineer,' turned and walked back to his car.

Her cap clenched in her hands, Rennie went inside as he drove off and threw herself face down on the bed. All the trouble she had gone to, to show nothing of her personal feelings! The pains she had taken to lose herself in the business of drilling and blasting and maintaining complicated machinery in the rough and tough environment of the mine. And she had been doing fine until Todd Dillman had come along!

CHAPTER FOUR

'IF you blow that thing up any higher it will burst and we'll all go up in smoke!' Sylvia Crowther, the mine manager's wife, laughed as her small son pumped furiously at a rubber animal which had known better days at the beach.

Leo was five and just learning to do things for himself. His brother Curtis, a lusty eight-year-old, and sister Dory, going on for eleven, were half strangling a white rabbit which, tolerantly indifferent to their fondling, preferred to hop about twitching his nose ecstatically at the garden shrubbery. The Crowthers had two older daughters who were away at college in Pretoria.

Rennie wriggled her bare feet in the cool grass and let Sylvia's chatter wash over her. The mine manager's house, overlooking the main gates of the mine, was large and comfortable. She felt completely relaxed here. All the family were easy-going and friendly. The children wore the American-styled nebbed golfing caps to shade their eyes from the sun and no one thought it odd that she wore her hair coiled up beneath similar headgear.

Sylvia was a woman approaching middle age, but with plenty of help in the house she had managed to hold on to her smart appearance. Brown-haired and vivacious, she was not too wrapped up in her home and family to forget that there was an intriguing world outside. Martin, her husband, was a thick-set, greying-haired man with a kindliness hidden away beneath his tough managerial exterior.

The couple had welcomed Rennie on her arrival and she had since become part of the household. Its warmth was a kind of escape from the desolate feel of her working quarters. If Martin had any thoughts on the peculiarities of her occupation he kept them to himself, and as she didn't come under his jurisdiction at the mine they never discussed work.

He sat now in shorts and shirt with his bare feet thrust into a pair of old leather sandals, browsing lazily through the Sunday papers. One might have believed that he was half-way towards dozing off, then a snippet of information would catch his interest and he would read it out aloud for the benefit of the other loafers in the garden. No one paid much attention, not even when at one point, after turning a page, he adjusted his reading glasses to announce, 'It says here that a diamond weighing ninety-two carats has been found at the Kerbrucken mine in South West Africa.'

Dislodging a toy gardening tool from beneath the small of her back where she lay, Rennie asked idly, 'Is that a record?'

'The only one I can recollect approaching that size was the one found at Hopetown near Kimberley around a century ago, eighty-three and a half carats. A smaller one of twenty-one carats was considered a find before that.'

Reaching out to re-do the back buttons of Dory's dress, Sylvia slanted a long-suffering though affectionate look at her husband and told Rennie, 'Martin worked as a boy at the Kimberley diamond mine, and he never lets us forget it.'

'But what about the big, *big* diamond you found once, Dad?' Curt flattened the rabbit as he sprawled to stop it hobbling off.

'The Cullinan?' Martin sloped a smile at his son. 'I didn't exactly find it, old chap. It was quite a bit before my time. About my only claim to a share in its fame is that I worked with the grandson of Sam Wells, the surface mana-ger of the Premier mine in those days, who discovered it lodged in a side wall of the open mine. He saw something reflecting the rays of the setting sun, climbed up and pulled it out with his bare hands. That's the way I had it told to me.'

'Was it really, really big?' Dory asked, balancing on one

leg with fierce concentration as though she had heard the story many times before.

'Weighed over three thousand carats,' her father told her. 'And if you go to London you'll see the Star of Africa and other gems cut from the Cullinan diamond in the British Crown Jewels.'

The information did nothing to stir anyone greatly. They might have been discussing the price of vegetables at the Vukasi roadside store instead of one of the most fantastically valuable minerals of the earth. Perhaps, like bank employees who are surrounded by money all day long, they viewed diamonds as an ordinary commodity to them because they lived and worked within sight and sound of their recovery.

For Rennie at any rate, the subject was a little too close to home. It reminded her of the dust and clatter she would have to face early the following morning. She didn't want to think of work just now, not with the bowl of blue sky above her and the dabs of white clouds and the birds, flashes of brilliant colour as they skimmed through her line of vision to perch noisily in the tambouti trees on the edge of the garden.

Someone else who wasn't remotely interested in the gem trade was young Leo. His face, flushed and mischievous, was the next thing to plop into her view from above. He complained gigglingly as she tickled his ribs, 'I'm hungry.'

'That makes two of us.' His mother hoisted him up and dropping a smacking kiss on his plump cheek gave the word to the others, 'Lunch should just be about ready.'

After a tasty meal of Transvaal-style sausages, farm-cured bacon, potted cheese, butter-cake and fruit, Rennie played games with the children. The older two went to school in the mine settlement and at the moment were fired with enthusiasm for the national gymnastics shortly to be held in Pretoria. Curt fancied himself on the horizontal bar and wobbled on a mop handle across the lawn flexing his muscles. Dory was lost in the business of practising the splits and in between pushing the placid Leo on the garden swing Rennie tried to help out with advice.

After a while she left them to it and drifted towards the house for a drink. Sylvia was just coming out of the front door and eyeing her fresh, groomed look in flowered dress, Rennie said with a smile, 'It looks as though someone's going out.'

'The du Preez are giving a cocktail party this afternoon.' The older woman's dark eyes sparkled with anticipation. Pulling on her white gloves, she said, 'Why don't you come along? Nobody minds gatecrashers out here, and it will give you a chance to get to know some of the others in the community.'

Rennie hesitated. She really hadn't planned to do much socialising in the settlement. Martin, sitting unkempt and relaxed in a deckchair on the porch, obviously avoided these affairs, but he was wise enough to know that his wife, with her warm nature and avid interest in people, thrived on anything that made a change from day-to-day routine.

He said to Rennie with an ominous gleam, 'And nobody misses a gatecrasher, if you want to leave. Give it a try. You might even enjoy yourself.'

Well, why not! His encouraging grin decided her. She was wearing royal blue slacks and shirt, and all it needed was a wash and freshen up. Within a few minutes they were saying goodbye to the children and pulling away in Sylvia's cream sports car.

As they started to climb the older woman said with wry humour, 'Cars are rather superfluous around the settlement. The men don't need them, and in any case employees are not allowed to take them into the diamond mine compound, and every house is within walking distance of the main gates.'

Rennie smiled. 'It's nice to arrive in style, even if one is only going a few yards,' she said, eyeing the somewhat opulent dwellings along the roadside. From below they had looked much the same as the neat bungalows inside the compound, but at close quarters it was easy to see by the lush stretches of garden and grand entrances that this was the 'Nob Hill' district of the Vukasi mine settlement.

'That's what I say.' Sylvia swung the wheel past perfumed banks of flowers. 'And it's handy to be able to take off to town occasionally.' She must have felt that her remark needed explaining, for she went on in cheerful vein, 'I'm used to it. I've lived this way since the day I was married, and with Martin's position I'm fortunate in having the job of entertaining and putting up the various officials who come to Vukasi. But some of the younger wives find the narrow confines of mining life a bit hard to take at times. They drive over to Wykveld or Tombaza to get away, and sometimes as far as Pretoria when the mood takes them.'

'That must be quite a ride from all the way up here in the wilds,' Rennie commented.

'It is, but it's fun,' Sylvia said with her unbridled zest for living. 'The company pays for the girls to be flown home from college during the holidays, but I've made the trip down once or twice to pick them up, just for something to do. Here we are.' She drove in between wide gates and exclaimed at the clutter of cars in the drive, 'It looks as though we've got a few city guests here today.'

The residence, a sizeable bungalow, clung to the side of the hill. Its garden was mainly rockery, a blaze of cascading cactus flowers. The view must have been considerable, but there was no time to turn and look, for Sylvia, her face alight with piquant anticipation, was making for the indoors.

The noise was a little unnerving—loud laughter and the drone of voices giving the impression that the house was bursting at the seams with guests. It wasn't quite as bad as that, but the spacious lounge where Sylvia led the way seemed to be draped with people. She was the kind of woman who blended in immediately with her surroundings and in no time at all was chatting away to one or another of those she knew. Rennie, feeling ill at ease, was introduced around and had her hand taken here and there in a form of insipid welcome, but nobody wanted to break off their conversations, which seemed to be all about the latest shows and current celebrities to be found in the nightclubs and restaurants of Johannesburg.

She met Angela du Preez, a tall woman of about thirty, looking very soignée in a velvet blouse and slim skirt. As the hostess she made a show of polite interest on hearing that they had a newcomer to the Vukasi mine settlement.

'Rennie has only been with us a short time,' Sylvia, blithely ignorant of the woman's patronising air, informed her juicily. 'Guess what she is!' And with a proud smile Rennie's way, 'She's an engineer.'

'How unusual.' Angela contributed a warmed-up smile and waved a languid arm. 'Help yourself to a drink, and do feel at home among the crowd.' After which she floated off to another part of the room.

Undaunted, Sylvia took up a conversation with their nearest neighbour and Rennie, glass in hand, and apparently part of the group, was able to withdraw and take stock of her surroundings. Here was a scene totally different from the rough-and-tumble get-together of the mining technicians at Todd's house yesterday. On the hillside lived the men with highly trusted positions at the mine, executives with key jobs in the sorting house where the diamonds were sorted by hand and in other security sections. They talked together in a group at the far end of the room, city men in expensive suits or fashionable sporting attire, misfits in a rough mining community but necessary for its survival.

Their wives, equally sophisticated but with little rapport with the isolated high-veld conditions, were making the most of the 'foreign element' in the room—young men who had driven up for the day, friends and friends of friends, who in a reverse sort of way were hungry for excitement.

Rennie smiled gloomily to herself at her observations. Was anyone ever entirely happy with his lot? She realised too, not without a trace of wryness, that though she did a man's job and was dressed not unlike the Adonis types who were temporarily relieving the wives' boredom, she didn't quite fit the bill when it came to being included. Had Rennie known it she was far too shapely a figure to have been invited over.

She saw Darrell Timpson among the group. He gave her a wave and a smile, but nothing more to say they had spent the best part of a morning together driving to Wykveld and back. She could have felt hurt if she hadn't recognised the fact that Darrell, lost as he was out here, was the type who needed the maternal company of old women.

Slightly apart now from Sylvia's group, she was able to give her attention to the view from the window. It was fascinating though not terribly awe-inspiring, for spread out below was the whole mining complex. She could see the workers' habitations, rows and rows of little pillboxes in postage-stamp gardens over a mile-wide stretch and the shops and community buildings with their surrounding furls of green in the centre. From up here it was rather like a neatly woven carpet which had been laid down with precision on the rough, parched veld. And over in the far distance, linked by an arrow-straight main road, was the mining area, an ugly stretch of quarried earth and rock and adjoining work buildings.

'There you see it, warts and all.' Sylvia, who was too nice a person to neglect her for long, came to join her, and when she had exchanged Rennie's glass for a fuller one began to make conversation on the various members of the gathering. 'You see the tall, balding man talking with Jack du Preez, that's Frank Markson, chief of administration. And John Spruyt—he's the one with the spectacles near the door— works in the central treatment plant. So many you haven't met yet. Oh, and the redhaired young man in the corner.

When we get a chance I'll introduce you. You and he are about the same age and . . .'

'I've already met Darrell,' Rennie said with a smile.

'Oh, you have. Good!' Sylvia took a sip of her drink and sighed. 'He's quite a pleasant boy, but something of a problem. I don't think he's cut out for the rough work and from what Martin says nothing else seems to suit him. There was talk of having to send him back home, but Todd Dillman, he's the man we take our troubles to while Mr Kramer is away—I don't know whether you've run into him yet——'

'I've run into him,' Rennie said succinctly.

'Well, Todd talked Martin into trying him out in other jobs to give him time to adjust to the life. Now you see the couple making for the terrace—well, Otto, that's Sophie's husband, is a descendant of the Kroondalers. There's a German hamlet driving west from . . .'

Rennie, though apparently paying attention, was inwardly detached and soon became lost in her thoughts. So Darrell hadn't been kicked out on his ear as he might have been in any other mining company, she mused. Yet Todd had given no hint of his leniency when they talked yesterday. Was that a side of him she didn't know?

With the drinks flowing free and young blood in from the city, the atmosphere of the party was reaching a pitch where just to stand around and chat was being considered tame. Feats of balancing soda syphons topped by unwieldy columns of glasses on raised knees were being attempted and one of the wives was causing a stir by doing a waltz on the grand piano. It was all rather like the eve-of-term blow-out with the mining executive couples playing the students, eager to make the most of their freedom before classes started the following day.

When the word suddenly went up that there was to be a motor-cycle work-out at the tailings dump, the response to transfer at once to the mine compound was noisily unanimous. Rennie had completely forgotten her promise to

Leith. As she drifted uncertainly with the rush Sylvia urged her on and gave her a wave. 'Go along and have fun. It's time I was getting back to the children.'

Outside she piled into someone's car which followed the procession down to the main gates. Though the executives held a certain amount of sway at the mine there was no question of waving aside security measures for their convenience. The town guests all thought it was highly amusing that they were searched *before* they went into the diamond mine compound. The others knew the drill and to them it was a minor inconvenience on the way to the entertainment ahead. They had to take what mine transport was available out to the tailings dump.

The place had all the appearance of a motor-cycle grand prix when they arrived. The mounds of a kind of hardened slag, discarded waste from the quarry, made an ideal surface for this sort of machine and several of the enthusiasts were testing conditions over the circuit which had been marked out with crudely coloured posts and oil drums.

Near the pipe-line sheds other boiler-suited figures were checking over their bikes. Leith was there and Zach the Shangaan, and one or two from the bore-hole unit. These were the men who used their spare time at the isolated up-country mine in another way. No pseudo-enjoyment for them. They had built their machines with loving care and the test would be who had made the best job of it.

Rennie left the spectators and joined the bike crew. She felt more useful there and it must be admitted more at ease. She borrowed a pair of dungarees and the men welcomed her noisily, for wasn't she one of them? They all considered her a kind of lucky charm and she was kept busy joining them in the last-minute tinkering touches to their handi-work. Leith, of course, thought she had planned the visit especially to cheer him on. And in her smile she gave no indication of the fact that she had forgotten all about the race and might never have appeared if she hadn't been more or less hijacked down there. Big and uncouth, he proudly pointed out to her his latest gadgets with his great oily hands. She was obliged to join him in the tightening up of various sections.

With the revving up of engines and the frequent test runs taking place there was an air of gay expectancy about the scene. The spectators, elegantly dressed wives now oblivious to the slag dust and the fumes, anything for a change, were waving scarves and dress sashes and noisily demanding action, and the men tossed hoots and catcalls at the competitors, just to make things lively.

Joking with Leith and pitching in with the odd adjustment, Rennie knew nothing of the additional arrivals on the scene until a stir of another nature caused her to lower her spanner. When she looked up it was to see Todd and Lila Harwood being greeted as they trotted up on horseback. For some reason her heart started to bang idiotically against her ribs. It was only a few hours since she had seen Todd late the previous afternoon, yet her breath came in painful little spurts in her throat.

If the atmosphere had been laughingly keyed-up before it was slightly inflammable now. Lila seemed to have that effect on people. Dashing in a white trouser suit, a red bandana tied round her russet-gold hair, she slid to the ground amid welcoming cheers and general frivolity. New faces in the mine settlement were avidly sought out, but Lila with her goldmine-owning father and appetite for adventure was obviously doubly popular with the thrill-starved group.

The horses were led away to a more peaceful spot and Todd strolled in, to be greeted heartily by the men. Rennie busied herself with her spanner. She had never expected him to turn up here, and trust her to be greased up and smeared with oil! In fawn shirt and riding breeches he eyed her across the space, his glance idly mocking as it locked with hers and then trailed over Leith making no end of a din with his engine beside her.

But it was Lila who led the way over to admire the chief engineer's handiwork. Her cold fawn eyes were over-bright, the smell of gasoline and exhaust fumes seemed to act like alcohol in her veins. She said with an accusing pout once the racket had subsided, 'Leith, you've no right to be riding so magnificent a machine when all I have is a four-legged beast.'

'Why didn't you bring your Porsche 2000 down here?' he grinned.

'Company rules,' Lila sighed. She cast aside thoughts of her fast racing car and fingered the chrome-work of the bike, querying with a sardonic look at Rennie. 'Don't tell me our little grease monkey friend here has had a hand in its construction?'

'Leith built it all by himself,' Rennie corrected smoothly. 'I couldn't very well claim any of the honours for simply tightening up a few nuts.'

'Don't insult the lady,' Todd, with his ironic expression, put in. 'There's a world of difference between a mechanic and an engineer.'

Rennie smiled thinly. If he looked at her like that much more she was sure she would hit him! She replied obliquely, 'In some cases we mix it. Leith here shines at most masculine professions.'

Lila looked at them both in turn and lifted an amused eyebrow at Rennie. 'Still breathing fire because the men won't accept you?' And at Todd, 'Why don't you leave the girl to her slide rules and turbines?'

'Gladly.' His smile was tight. 'I only rib the lipstick and lace types.'

Lila hardly heard. She was eyeing the motor-bike covetously. Astride it, the chief engineer invited jokingly, 'Hop on. See how she feels.'

'Don't tempt me, Leith,' Lila laughed. 'It wouldn't be the first time I've ridden one of those things, you know.'

'In that case she's all yours.' He dismounted. 'The engine needs a work out anyway.'

Lila was astride in a moment. In control now of the machine, she registered a look of brittle exhilaration. Revving up, she called above the noise, 'How do I look, Todd?'

'It's your neck,' he said drily.

Watching all that was going on, the spectators were in a ferment seeing Lila's white-clad figure crouched low over the thundering construction of gleaming metal. It was something like this they had been waiting for. Surging forward, they went wild as she took off towards the sloping course offering shouts of encouragement, whistles and cheers. Rennie had to admire the woman's superb handling of the cumbersome giant. Once away she leapt up and over the series of hummocks with a kind of flamboyant majesty and ice-cool nerve which was quietly staggering. Out on the flat she opened up to a breathtaking speed, flying over the ground until it did indeed seem as though she had wings.

The bedlam from the onlookers was deafening. All eyes were fixed on the speeding shape. Someone had a pair of field glasses and as they went the rounds Rennie had them thrust into her hands from a cheering neighbour. She soon picked up the hurtling figure. But it was Lila's face brought up close by the powerful lenses which held her attention. Lovely still in a detached way, her features had become a marble mask lit only by the ecstasy of speed.

She was on the home run in a matter of minutes and thundering towards the onlookers as they went crazy to welcome her in. It said something for the fabulous Lila's ride when her red bandana was still firmly in place and apart from a little cinder dust her tailored white trouser suit had emerged unmarked. But she wasn't the type to bask over-long in adulation. Once she had handed the bike over she seemed to lose that vital spark which had been so noticeable only seconds before. It was as though the life in her had suddenly been switched off. In a way she was so like the machines she hungered after, bursting with dynamic power and sparkling performance and then nothing. Rennie watched her beside Todd with not so much as a quiver about her smile. Was that how he liked his women, full of sangfroid and emotionless?

After Lila's stunning performance the actual race was something of an anti-climax. The competitors were cheered at the start and whistled at on their way over the bumps, but interest flagged after a while and as the distance consisted of several laps the riders were left to fight it out for themselves.

Besides, Todd was the chief attraction now for the executives' wives. While Lila chatted indifferently around, her male companion was claimed as the main event of the afternoon. Rennie thought she would give him a bit of his own back and eyed him with outrageous raillery as he stood among the fawning women. As usual he handled it all with maddening panache, lingering just long enough over each conversation and rooting the females with his rather devastating smile.

With the roar of the bikes on the final approach enthusiasm kindled again to greet the victor. Out of the half dozen or so competitors four managed to finish the race. Leith was the winner, which was no surprise to Rennie. After all, she mused humorously, he had put much of his time in during working hours perfecting his machine, and who was to say that it hadn't been endowed with a special kind of magic having first been ridden by the dazzling Lila!

Of course she, as his chief co-worker, made a great fuss of the champion on his arrival. Many of the mining crew and their mates were there and Leith was embraced and toasted with freshly opened cans of beer, and Rennie, in the thick of it, effusively congratulated the chief engineer on his daring achievement. Like Todd with his languishing admirers she too could lay it on thick when she wanted to, and just for good measure she smiled widely and planted a kiss prettily on Leith's cheek.

Someone had fashioned a crude flower chain out of wild aloes and it was Rennie's job to place this ceremoniously around Leith's neck, while cameras clicked to record the hilarious event, for the benefit of relatives and friends at home. Snuggled against Leith to make a fitting pose for the photographers, Rennie ran up against Todd's gaze, which was expressive in its whimsical disdain.

It was getting dark when the meeting finally broke up. With talk of 'chow' the bike crowd drifted off towards the residential compound in search of a meal. But the hillside group, loth to return to the comparative quiet of the mine settlement, were still in party mood and raring to go when someone suggested doing the thirty-mile drive into town. It was only when she had consented to accept a lift that Rennie saw Lila and Todd cantering off on their own towards the main gates. She wondered then what had made her agree to join up with the others.

The evening was not unpleasant. Rennie was partnered by a young man who worked as a hotel receptionist in Johannesburg and the night life of Wykveld, though limited, made a change from the mine compound. Yet when she had been dropped off in the early hours and was making her way to her bungalow, she asked herself why the outing had somehow fallen flat. Was it because Todd had been missing from the group?

CHAPTER FIVE

THE next morning in the pearly grey light of dawn Rennie rose unrested from her bed and stumbled down to the workshed to pick up her conveyance. Wryly she cast her mind back to the night before. Well, at least she had got to know how the other half of the mine settlement lived, but she doubted whether she would be repeating the experience.

Out at the quarrying site everything seemed to go wrong that day. There was a collision between an electric shovel and a giant excavator. Luckily no one was hurt, but there was the tangle of machinery to be unravelled. Then the steel entry shaft at the crushing plant caved in. A call was put out for the chief engineer, but as he failed to materialise it was left to Rennie to issue what instructions she thought fit. Shouting to the men working the temporary crane, she quietly fumed. Leith was the end! He was never there when she needed him. Surely he wasn't tinkering with his motorbike now when he had proved its worth? More than likely he was snoring on his bunk after too big a lunch.

By late afternoon her spirits had lifted a little. They were almost through another working day and soon she would be able to retire to the seclusion of her own quarters. A warm shower and an early night would put her right.

It was about a fortnight later when she was driving back from the mining site one evening that she saw a station wagon parked outside the engineer's office. Her breathing was slightly irregular as she swung the range truck into the shed and walked across the space to the grass enclosure. Inside Todd's presence twanged at her pulses, but she gave the impression of hardly noticing him as she went straight to the drawer of the desk.

'Sorry we don't cater for visitors,' she said offhandedly,

tossing in her keys. 'If you're going to make a habit of dropping in, I'll see about having an armchair delivered.'

'The desk's okay, thanks,' he said, oozing his usual self-assurance and swinging a suede-shoe-clad foot from where he was draped on its corner. 'When I want extra padding I'll bring my own.' Over his open-necked shirt he was wearing a light windcheater to combat the chill evening air and the width of him seemed to take up all the available breathing space. Without stirring he fixed his green gaze on Rennie and asked lazily, 'How's the job going?'

'Fine, thank you.' Jerkily she brushed a tendril of hair from her tired brow.

'No problems?'

'No, why should there be?' She tried to sound light-hearted.

'You're looking a bit peaky.' Though his whole mood was playful she felt ridiculously hurt that it had to be him who should notice that she wasn't looking her best.

She said with unnecessary acid, 'I'm not fortunate enough to be able to spend my time hanging around the mine compound like some people.'

He rose leisurely and smilingly impervious to her barbed remark thrust his hands into his pockets. 'I really came to give you some news.' And after a pause, 'Coulton Kramer, the mine owner, is coming back. He'll be flying in some time tomorrow.'

Rennie lifted her gaze from the work sheet in her hand. 'Does that mean we'll be seeing the back of you?'

'Afraid so,' he grinned at her.

She ticked off one or two names with a flair and turning to another job remarked breezily, 'That's the best news I've had in weeks.'

'Don't be too sure.' Todd moved with her, wearing a lazy smile. 'You haven't met Coult yet.'

'I'll take my chances any day with the true boss of the

mine,' Rennie said sweetly. 'At least it won't be a case of fencing with shadows.'

'Is that the only impression I've made?' He faced her and gleamed idly, letting her know that he was very real substance. She felt her heart suddenly start to thump and drifted to a less suffocating part of the office.

He stayed until it was time to lock up, nodding to the men who came to hand in their chits at the window and generally getting in the way. She closed up the pigeonhole window at last and gathered up her things from the desk. Todd was ahead of her. He opened the door for her with a sweeping gesture and when they were out on the road he asked with a lopsided smile, 'Care for a lift?'

'I like to walk home after the day's work,' Rennie replied without stopping. 'There's nothing like a good blow for getting rid of the mine dust and other irritants.'

He shrugged equably, 'Don't say I didn't offer.'

Thankfully she heard him stroll away to his car and drive off. But when he had gone she felt flat and deflated.

With work at the diamond mine continuing as normal no one paid much attention to the owner's return. Rennie saw the private jet as it came in to land behind the hill settlement, but she was busy out on the north side of the quarry and soon forgot about it.

The first indication she had of Coulton Kramer's arrival was one afternoon some days later when the mine manager's Landrover came cruising towards the kimberlite terrace where work was in progress. Beside the site office Martin stepped out and with him was an elderly man of slender build with a shock of white hair and craggy features. There was nothing in his appearance to suggest that he was one of the richest men in the world except that his cavalry twill trousers were of an excellent cut and the fawn cardigan he wore despite its being a hot day was of finest wool.

Leith happened to be fully occupied at that moment un-ravelling the cable of the rotary bucket excavator which was always seizing up. He came to sort out a mighty wrench and stopped briefly with his big smile. 'Great to see you back, boss.'

'Good to be here, Leith. Good to be back home,' he slapped the colossal shoulder as it went by. Then as the mine manager preceded him, 'And who's this?'

Rennie, her dungarees caked with dust and her peaked cap awry, met his gaze then. His eyes, which were a washed-out blue, had the piercing quality of ice peaks with frosty sun on them.

'Rennie's our second engineer,' he was told. 'She started a few days after you left.'

'I see.' He made no move to acknowledge her, except to say, 'Odd job for a girl, isn't it?'

'She's a good worker,' Martin smiled at Rennie. 'We have no complaints.'

'Isn't that Freddie Madula you've got on the bedrock slicer?' The mine owner passed on and Rennie felt as though an arctic wind had just blown by.

Busy as she was, the incident was soon blotted from her mind, but a long time later when Martin and the mine owner were driving away a curious apprehension fell over her; a faint little stir of unease inside her which she couldn't shake off despite the fact that work was going with a swing and the sun shone down gloriously from a cloudless blue sky.

Leith was in his usual joking mood and she played along with him, telling herself that it was pure feminine imagina-tion. There was not a thing in the air except the fresh, sharp tang of the open veld and the hot, heady perfume of sweet thorn hardly marred by the acrid dust of the quarry.

They got the excavator going again and later enjoyed themselves stripping down a faulty geological sounder on a grassy patch within sight of the pick crews' pantomiming as they chipped away at the kimberlite pipe.

Rennie had forgotten all about her earlier uneasiness when the time came to knock off work for the day. Swinging along the road to her bungalow after locking up the office, she promised herself a tepid shower, a change of clothing and a deckchair on the lawn. The nights were summery now and there was time for an hour or two out of doors before darkness brought the cold.

She had brushed her hair out blissfully after it had been clogged under her cap all day and was zipping up clean denims over a pale blue tee-shirt when a noise outside drew her to the window. No one ever came this way. Hers was the end one in a line of empty bungalows—bachelors were few in Vukasi—and she never saw a vehicle on the road from one week to the next. But there was one there now, an old mine conveyance, shuddering with its engine still running as though the driver had little time to waste.

She hurried to the door. It was Romaano, one of the gardeners, on the path. She had seen him often tending the roses and palm plants outside the compound supermarket. His coal-black features were merrily alert as she met him and he doffed his cap. 'Mr Kramer sent me. He wants to see you.'

'What, now?' Rennie looked slightly stupid.

'That's what he said. He stopped me and said to go to number ninety-seven, the last hut on E block. And missie, I think that's you.'

'Yes, that's me.' Rennie felt the uneasiness stir in her again. 'But where do I go? Has he got an office or something?'

'Dunno 'bout n'office, but his house is out past the north avenue. I cleaned up the grounds there yesterday.'

She didn't know it, but she would find it. Romaano shuffled his white-plimsolled feet, itching to be off. His working day was no longer than hers. She thanked him for the message and sent him on his way. As he drove off she started out on foot. It was necessary to go down and pick up the range truck. Apparently the mine owner lived at the opposite end of the compound to where her own accommodation was situated. And from what she had seen of him this morning, she thought later as she drove out towards the north road, it was maybe just as well. Strange that he didn't live in the hill settlement where the trusted executives' homes added a touch of luxury to the scene. But if he liked privacy as they said he did perhaps he felt more of a recluse *inside* the barbed wire. That he was wily there was no doubt. She noticed he had summoned her in her own time, not his.

The road, like all the other avenues in the compound, was ruler-straight, and passing several blocks of red-roofed hostels and bungalows Rennie came at last to the extreme outer edge of the residential quarter. Here indeed was wilderness. The road ended abruptly and was lost in semi-desert and coarse vegetation which seemed to stretch for miles into the hazy distance. There was a dusty track at right angles, however, and this led to a walled-in residence, conspicuous in its isolation in the midst of grassy wastes.

Well, here goes! Rennie made straight for the forbidding gateway. Mr Kramer wanted to see her, so here she was. A little pulse began to work at the base of her throat. Whatever it was that was on his mind, she might as well get it over with.

She opened the gates herself as there appeared to be no one about and drove in boldly. The grounds were pretty in a sparse way with lawns and flowering shrubs, but the house was little more than a works bungalow except that it was larger and more sprawling and had a veranda with potted greenery along it.

She parked just inside the gates and walked the rest of the way. No one came to greet her and as the front door was open there was nothing to do but go inside. The spacious interior was comfortably but simply furnished.

Rennie was gathering a hazy impression of upholstered canework armchairs, woven floormats and tawny lampshades when a voice from over by the windows said harshly, 'So you're here at last?'

Coulton Kramer was stood with his back to her beside a writing desk. He wore spectacles and was scanning the book in his hand in the evening sunlight. Rennie said, fuming quietly at his rudeness, 'I came as soon as I got your message.' She might as well have spoken to the carved wood cheetah stood grinning at her from beside the doorway for all the reaction she got.

When he had fully satisfied himself with the contents of the book the mine owner tossed it down with a clunk on the desk and turned. He took his time in removing his spectacles, folding them methodically and placing them in a metalled case which he afterwards thrust securely into the pocket of his cardigan. Rennie had plenty of time to study him while all this was taking place. She assessed his age at somewhere in the early sixties; although he was physically ravaged by the illnesses he had suffered it was possible he was younger. He was still a fine-looking man despite his stooped shoulders and fleshless features, but of temperament that was another matter. As she was beginning to discover, that was something which hardened his expression to the quality of granite.

He moved towards the centre of the room to get a clearer view of her and asked, 'How long have you been practising your engineering gimmicks around the mine complex?'

She noticed the suggestion of a drawl in his speech, also the steely sarcasm. 'All in all about a month, I think,' she replied evenly.

He nodded, the death knell in his sneer as he swept her with that arctic glance. 'I don't know how you got into my outfit, but I intend to make damn sure you don't stay.'

Well, here it was! Rennie had sensed it ever since their

earlier meeting. She said stiffly, 'Do you have a reason for your decision?'

'You bet I have,' he snapped, wagging a finger at her. 'You're a female, and I don't hold with females fooling around in places they don't belong.'

'Are you dissatisfied with my work?' Rennie asked levelly.

'That's not the point. Mining for diamonds is a highly skilled business and no woman is going to meddle with expensive machinery of mine when I've got trained men for the job.'

'Surely that's sexual discrimination?' Rennie said coolly.

'You're blamed right, it's sexual discrimination. And I make the laws around here.' Still jabbing his finger at her, he began to pace stormily. 'Now listen to me, young woman. Don't come to me with your high-falutin' modern ideas. I'll tell you why I practise discrimination of the sexes, because they're different, that's why. A man's built of brawn and muscle to help him cope with the conditions of his daily life. A woman's soft and made for having babies, and the fact that she fancies herself wearing a steel helmet and swinging a hammer ain't gonna change things.'

Rennie agreed. Oh, how she agreed! But what could she do? What would her father say if she lost her job? With a bitter smile she could see him now striding about. He would be inconsolable. The image made her draw herself up and argue boldly, 'It seems to me that you're not so much interested in what's best for your mine machinery as cussedly standing in the way of progress.'

'Progress, ha!' He eyed her with blistering scorn. 'I can tell you something about that too. I treat my workers with more trust and confidence than a lot of other mine operators. My boys can bring their families into the compound, they don't get X-rayed every time they go out of the main gates and they can quit any time they want to. Yessir, the Kramer diamond mine is one of the most forward-seeing outfits in the whole of the Union, and don't you forget it.'

Rennie trembled inwardly at his thunderous mood, but she put on an appearance of wooden indifference. She mustn't allow him to break her with his fiery bombast. *She mustn't.* Her anger held in check until now, she said spiritedly, 'I'm not denying that your mine compounds are admirably run, but that doesn't mean that there isn't room for changes. I'm a fully qualified engineer and I refuse to believe that you can't use my services just because of some stupid dogmatic principle.'

'Oh, you do! Well, perhaps you didn't hear me right, young lady——'

As they faced each other across the room the attention of both was distracted by the sound of a car speeding into the grounds. It pulled up with a jerk outside the house. There were swift footsteps on the veranda and in came Todd. His sharp glance swung from Rennie to Coulton Kramer, noting the warlike atmosphere. He said to the mine owner, 'Martin's just told me the facts. I suppose he explained that we neither of us felt qualified to interfere with the launching of the new engineer in case you'd okayed the thing before you left.'

'Me!' The older man made a gesture of sizzling disgust. 'The day I start a woman is the day you can put me six feet under.'

'You're going to outlive us all, Coult,' Todd said with a grin. He relaxed his frame as he strolled in and asked casually, 'What's the problem, anyway?'

The mine owner glowered and waved a hand in exasperation. 'Todd, you're talking to me about problems when a chit of a girl stands here and insists she's capable of doing a job as good as a man.'

'Not just as good, sometimes better,' Rennie put in unflinchingly. 'And I'm not a chit of a girl. I'm twenty-two years of age.'

'You see what I mean!' The mine owner's eyebrows shot up in irate amazement at the underling's audacity. 'She's convinced the company's going to fall apart without her.'

Todd said lazily, 'She might have a point, Coult. The pressure's been building up since you stepped up the earth-moving production to three hundred and fifty carats a day.'

'Don't tell me you're in cahoots with her,' the older man growled. 'I can have a mine engineer flown up here in a couple of days and you know it.'

'Why go to the trouble?' Todd said easily. 'No one's voiced any grumbles as to her capabilities as an engineer.'

'No. Well, I'm doing that right now!' the mine owner snorted.

'So I'm not to be judged on my work but on old-fashioned sentiment,' Rennie spoke up with withering calm. 'Well, since we're on the subject of the superior sex,' she eyed Coulton Kramer levelly—what had she to lose now, only her neck—'let me see you strip down an entire grease belt machine and put it back in working order again. And you——' she turned to Todd. Oh yes! He had done his share of labelling her incompetent. 'Could you dismantle a rotary scrubber and have it back in production in half an hour?' As he shot her a bemused look she added firmly, making it clear that she was referring to his intervention on her behalf, 'Thank you, but I don't need anyone to fight my battles for me.'

'The devil you don't!' For the first time she saw a crack in the mine owner's glowering exterior. With a spark of wicked humour in his glare he added, 'We've got to hand it to her, Todd. The girl's got grit.' The crack disappeared, to be replaced by iron sternness as he faced her. 'I suppose you know I could strip you of all your qualifications for this kind of insubordination. I'm the owner of a diamond mine, don't forget, and pretty powerful in these parts.'

'You couldn't strip me of my ability.' Rennie lifted her chin. 'And not all employers are bogged down in outdated ideas.'

She waited for the cannon salvo that would finish her, but there was nothing but a crackling silence. Then the mine owner shifted his gaze. 'What do you make of her, Todd? Put you in your place, didn't she?' he said with a chortle.

'She'll probably give you more trouble outside the mine compound than in it,' Todd said drily.

'I think you might be right.' Rennie was given the full benefit of his fierce twinkle. 'Old-fashioned, am I? Well, we'll see. For the time being I'll accept that you're an engineer, but I won't accept that you're anything more than a woman on any other count, so when the job gets too tough don't come to me.'

Rennie began to breathe again. 'I appreciate your change of heart,' she said primly.

'Heart! Don't talk to me about heart,' he was in his snorting mood again. 'Now go away,' he dismissed her with a wave of his hand and turned. 'Where the devil's Aaron with my night cap?'

'I'll go and stir him up,' Todd said with a soothing grin. 'I was just thinking it's time you were hitting the pillows.'

'Don't fuss me! I'm not senile yet. Give me a couple of days and I'll be making things hum around here.' Coulton Kramer looked back and wagged a finger at Rennie just sliding out of the door. 'And for your information, young lady, I was taking mine machinery apart when you were still in nappies.'

Phew! She made her way back to the range truck feeling limp. Now she knew both sides of the Kramer temperament—ice-cold indifference or blistering rage. But she had won. Yes, she had won. As she drove out of the gate there was no light of triumph in her eyes, just relief and a kind of weary acceptance.

She hadn't been cruising long on the road when she noticed Todd's car behind her. At first she thought he was on his way to the main gates, but as she swung to right and left along the avenues it soon became clear that he was tailing her back to her bungalow. Now what did he want? Rennie pushed a trembling hand through her hair. She had had enough of playing the dedicated engineer for one day. She didn't know whether she could cope with much more.

When they arrived she parked the range truck at the kerb and drifted over to the deck chair on the patch of lawn. A few seconds later Todd came to join her. He was wearing a suit of pale grey material and slackening his tie he hinted with a grin, 'Any drinks going? Thirsty work, cooling the old boy down.'

She indicated the door which she hadn't bothered to close. 'You'll find some Coca-cola in the kitchen.'

He grimaced. 'Nothing stronger? I thought tough engineers——'

Rennie went rigid. 'Now if you're going to start ...'

'Okay! Okay!' Repenting, he raised a hand at her stormy look. 'I'll settle for a Coke.' He went indoors and came out a few minutes later with two brimming glasses. Handing one to her, he dropped down to lounge on the step and smacked his lips appreciatively. 'Not bad if you hold your nose.'

'I happen to find it a very refreshing drink,' Rennie said, sipping decorously. She had to do something to still her wildly pumping heart. When she had been sitting the previous evening she had turned her chair away from the rays of the setting sun. Now, facing the steps, it was impossible to avoid the disturbing sight of Todd relaxing not far from her. In the rosy evening light he looked very tanned and his eyes, dark-lashed, were a clear, vibrant green in contrast.

With those eyes resting meditatively on her he said, 'You're a funny kid. Sitting there like a child at a tea party, and only ten minutes ago you were demanding to be equated with a man.'

'I was demanding to be allowed to keep my job,' she corrected.

'Is it so important?' His gaze narrowed. 'You were arguing back there as if your whole life depended on it.'

'Maybe it does,' she replied non-committally.

He threw back the rest of his drink, set his glass down and rose. 'You mean you'd never be able to show your face again at the Women's Lib movement.' His smile was tight with the old aggressive humour.

Rennie got up from her chair. 'It's getting chilly. I think I'll go in.'

'Oh no, you don't!' He hitched his trousers at the waist and flexed his shoulders. 'You may have got Coult believing that all useful work must be done with a sledge-hammer, but I happen to be harder to convince. In fact I'm going to turn the coin and show you the other side of a man's working day—mine, and there won't be a grease belt machine or a rotary scrubber in sight.'

'You did say work?' She couldn't help trying to pierce his smug self-assurance.

'That's right.' He didn't rise to the bait but merely gave her his shatter-proof smile. 'It's a question of brawn or brain.'

'And you men have got both?' she smiled acidly.

'I'll pick you up on Friday when you've knocked off work. Evening's the best time for viewing the grounds. No good in the sun's glare.'

'I can't wait.' She picked up the glasses and drifted indoors, hearing Todd move off to his car and drive away.

Work continued much the same as usual for the rest of the week. They saw nothing more of the mine owner at the

quarrying site and Leith drifted back to his old ways of
sliding off a job whenever he felt like it. But Rennie was
used to this by now. She had learned to cope reasonably
well on her own and in a way the chief engineer was doing
her a favour. Being left to it in the midst of a tricky situation might be exasperating, but it was one way of gathering
vital experience. Her major worry was that something too
big to handle would break while Leith was snoring away
the after-effects of drink on his bunk.

Most evenings she went to the Crowthers. There was
time for a romp with Curt and Dory in the garden before
they followed baby Leo to bed, then she and Sylvia and
Martin would sit with drinks on the front steps overlooking
the compound gates and lazily discuss life in the settlement.
The mine manager had not been able to contain his surprise at seeing Rennie still around after he had been
hauled over the coals that day by the mine owner. But she
smiled away her reinstatement and as it was a touchy subject with him he was happy enough not to have been involved in the outcome.

On Friday night Rennie locked up the engineer's office
and walked the short stretch to her bungalow. The heat of
the day still hung over the tawny-coloured landscape and
the low-lying blue mountains in the distance, but at the
roadside yellow and white daisies nodded contentedly in a
passing breeze and banks of periwinkles emanated their
cool green scent. Soothed as always by the wild beauty of
her surroundings, she was nevertheless slightly keyed-up.
Would Todd come for her as he had promised—or
threatened? She smiled wryly to herself when she recalled
that she had challenged him to match her capabilities as an
engineer. His male pride had been nicked and he was
interested solely in vindicating her on that point. In fact,
having cooled down since then he might not turn up at all.

Indoors she showered and changed into clean jeans and
a checked shirt, just in case, and coiled her hair under a

blue denim cap. Though she told herself that if Todd came it would be purely in an assertive mood she still couldn't stifle entirely this feeling of breathless expectancy.

CHAPTER SIX

RENNIE was flicking nonchalantly through a magazine on the lawn when he arrived. She had heard his car coming along the road and her heart had started its ridiculous thumping, but by the time he was stepping out at the kerb she had schooled herself into cool composure.

Casually dressed in white shirt and fawn slacks, he came to where she sat in the deck chair and gazing down at her his green eyes playful he asked, 'Ready?'

Smitten by his lighthearted mood, she queried innocently, 'Are we going somewhere?'

With a grin he led her to the car and seating her in front went round and took his place beside her at the wheel. When they were on the road he asked pleasantly, 'How was work today?'

'Fair,' Rennie shrugged. 'No major breakdowns, thank heaven.'

'Seen anything of your new boss, the mine owner?' he asked with humour.

'Not a sign,' she said with relief.

'I doubt whether you will.' Todd steered past the last of the bachelor residences and on towards the more lush-fronted bungalows. 'Coult is a strict recluse and hardly ever leaves his house. He has four private planes but seldom uses them and practically never receives visitors. His only hobby is books—first editions. He's got hundreds of them awaiting classification.'

'Strange why a man so rich should live so frugally,' Rennie mused.

'Money makes no difference to some people.' They cruised through the shopping area thronged with gaily decked-out African mine workers strolling with their wives and girl friends visiting for the week-end. 'Coult wanted to find diamonds and he found them. He was fanatically devoted to his cause and when he struck lucky I suppose everything else became a kind of anti-climax.'

'But it all seems such a waste. He wrecked his health and now all he does is hide himself away with his hobbies. He could have done that without the diamond hunt, surely?'

'Some men are like that. It's the thrill of the search that counts.'

Ted Mills of Security had waved them through the main gates and they were crunching along the earth road skirting the hill settlement. This was Rennie's favourite stretch of Vukasi. The luxuriant green drapes of the river trees, the smell of moist ground and thriving vegetation—it was all so different from the dry parched veld on the other side of the hill. In fact they might have been two different worlds. Here there was shade and the flash of jewel-like birds lent an exotic touch to the scene. Out there was nothing but miles of shimmering wastes and the harsh cry of predatory winged creatures.

They passed the village store, gaily displaying flowers and fruit and wooden beads to tempt the week-end visitor, and further on the farm lands where in the distance the black and white speckle of cows could be seen grazing on a green stretch.

The gates of Rosedale were open. Todd drove straight in and Rennie's immediate surprise was that she had never known that the house was built on a ridge below the settlement hillside. There was a striking drop beyond the far stoep which overlooked the extensive grounds.

It was a lovely old place, and not so forbidding on closer

inspection. Her view now as she stepped out of the car was of green-shuttered windows, wooded side balconies, a white baroque frontage and of course the shady stoep. She wondered which was Lila's room and if she were here now. Obviously there were servants indoors, as some of the windows were open and there was the whispered sounds of activity inside, but the circular stretch of drive was empty apart from Todd's car, so it appeared that Lila was in Johannesburg.

'The house was built in the 1800s in the Dutch style to suit high-veld conditions.' Todd took her arm as she gazed up. 'It was bought in 1950 by the state and turned into a museum, but it's a bit too far off the beaten track even for the average traveller. Wallace Harwood acquired it some time back. He'll probably retire here one day.'

The gold-mining magnate, Lila's father? Rennie lowered her gaze to a mauve-coloured shrub. Where would his daughter be then. Married to Todd?

'That's hemizgia. It thrives up here in the northern Transvaal.' He nodded to the bush and led her on. 'We plant everything, of course, with maintenance in mind.'

Rennie started the tour with a sceptical smile, which became more and more difficult to hold as they progressed. Never had she seen such beauty in a collection of trees—stately gums, pines, and many whose names were a mystery to her, or vistas framed so perfectly in their green frieze, of lilac hills and sienna bluffs and rolling plain.

'The job is to integrate successfully the existing legacy of semi-matures with new planting,' Todd told her. 'Also we try for aesthetic effects derived from shade and shadow, the interesting use of levels ...'

They wandered up and down connecting flights of steps, many charmingly curved and built in natural stone, to different-sized spaces resulting in small and large leafy outdoor rooms. There were places to sit and rest, yet all were related to make a perfect woodland whole without realising how individual were the parts.

They passed a toolhouse of new undressed stone which looked like a log cabin in the trees, then as they came to delightful sounds and fragrances Todd said, 'Water, the classical component in landscape design, enhances a garden. We've re-sited an old water-wheel which is still in working order and use an Egyptian *shaduf* contrivance for controlling water.'

The sight they came upon was enchanting, a sunken area lush with palms, trailing blossom and tinkling water. Further on among the trees a stream danced by uninhibited following its own course over rough stone and rockery. There was an abstract fountain in a secluded corner and then out on the flat a lily pond. From here Rennie gazed across lawns so smooth she doubted if they were real towards sculptured bushes and herbaceous borders.

Beside her Todd said, 'A good garden should flow, invite one to find out what's round the next corner. There's still a lot of wild ground to be tamed, but the aim is to have it all like this one day.'

'And only an expert would know how to blend the old with the new,' she pointed out with an acquiescent gleam.

'Only an expert like me,' he shrugged with his smile of outrageous self-assurance. But there was nothing assertive in his mood now and the old aggressive humour was only noticeable when he looked at her. She knew he had been watching her with a satirical slant to his mouth during their tour and though the loveliness of the wooded garden had smitten her to the heart she had tried to look impassive. Now, as they walked, passing flaming poinsettias and exotic proteas, his green glance was turned her way for so long she was prompted to ask, 'What are you looking at?'

'You,' he replied lazily. 'I was thinking of that time at my house when you almost wept at the beer stains on the carpet. And later when I caught you wandering through the rooms. You've got that same look on your face, like a child who's taken a peek at her party dress and mustn't let on.'

Rennie bit back her joy at the sight of a brilliant sun bird and said, faint colour in her cheeks, 'You're very analytical.'

'You bet.' He strolled idly alongside her, his mocking gaze unrelenting. 'If there was no one around now you'd be burying your face in the roses and tripping barefoot over the grass.'

She plucked a feathery strand in passing and twirling it asked lightly, 'What are you trying to prove?'

'That you're a lot more woman than you like to make out.'

Momentarily her blue glance met his green one, then smilingly skirting the thin ice she replied, 'A remark naturally designed to bolster your male ego, I bet!'

They came to the fountain on the terrace atop which cupids wrestled playfully with a goat, and some twenty feet below one could see a touch of the symmetrical approach where they had just walked, the lily pool, the lawns, the formal avenues.

Rennie turned her attention towards the house. She couldn't rid herself of the thought of Lila. Lila and Todd alone here in this paradise, wandering through the grounds together, perhaps sitting in one of those leafy alcoves in close embrace.

The effect of the vision was devastating. She had never known an emotion like this, like someone sawing through her insides with a jagged implement. Quickly she moved on.

It was Todd who pointed out the stables round the side of the house. The four-legged occupants became frisky and bright-eyed when they spotted the approaching company. Rennie patted the velvet-soft noses and watching her Todd said with his ever challenging grin, 'You ride, I suppose?'

Rennie hadn't been near a horse since she was fifteen, but her image as a tough engineer was at stake. 'Of course,' she replied unhesitant.

'Pick your mount,' he invited with a lazy smile. 'There's time for a sprint before dark.'

Rennie looked at the big black stallion and said off-handedly, 'I'll take Lila's horse. She won't mind, will she?'

'No.' Todd's laconic glance was mildly questioning. 'But Lucifer needs firm handling. He's used to going like the wind.'

Lucifer! The name should have been enough to warn her off, but a reckless desire to be as casually brilliant as Lila made her say confidently, 'I'll manage him all right.'

Todd saddled up and Rennie mounted. The stallion was as big as the side of a stable. She tried not to show her nervousness as they cantered out through the main gates. Out on the road Todd said, 'We'll make for the air strip and the veld beyond. It's good riding country.'

Good riding country! Rennie grasped the reins of her ebony steed, already well into his stride through no prompting from her. She certainly hoped so! But outwardly cool, she patted the straining black neck and called blithely, 'Let's go!'

Amazingly, once she was into the rhythm of the see-saw saddle an overwhelming exhilaration banished her fears. Lucifer's stride and pull was so tremendous as they approached the air strip she felt to be floating with the force of a rocket over the ground. It was all done so effortlessly with no urging on her part that she did indeed feel like the queen of speed. With the wind whistling past her ears, whipping the colour into her cheeks, the sparkle of excitement in her eyes, she had time to contemplate Todd racing alongside her. She saw how the gallop had brought a flush of dark red to his sunburnt features, heightening the whiteness of his smile, the ruggedness in him which she had always been aware of. She saw too as they plunged neck and neck towards open country that indolent gleam of his, challenging still.

Well, he would be the loser, she told herself with a laugh at the wind. His chestnut steed was a hardy horse, but obviously lacking Lucifer's power it must soon fall behind.

As she had expected, out on the open veld the stallion began to pull ahead. It was as though he knew exactly where he was going and needed no directions from her. Leaving Todd behind, what did she care? She was riding superbly, like Lila. And really there was nothing to it at all!

Streaking towards rough country, she thought she heard a shout from behind, but she ignored the impulse to turn. Lila would keep going. Lila would think of nothing but speed and more speed. Patches of thornveld flashed by, rocky outcrops. It was only when Lucifer veered wildly once or twice that she began to get the feeling that he didn't know where he was going at all. He was simply crazed with a longing for speed, just like his mistress. It had been built into him.

She decided it was time to slow down. She would let Todd catch her up and smile away her performance just like Lila would have done, knowing quietly that she was admired for her skill. She tugged at the reins, but if Lucifer recognised the signal he paid no heed to it. His mouth wide drinking in the pace, ignoring the bit, his nostrils flaring and steaming with excitement, he thundered on. Rennie tugged at the reins, having difficulty in keeping her seat as he plunged blindly on, stumbling over hummocks, rearing at obstacles but pounding, pounding ever onwards.

The ground was a blur beneath her and she felt her earlier fear of this big black prince of horses return. And that perhaps was her undoing. Her grip slackened as her nerve went, and Lucifer, uncertain suddenly, reared at full gallop and with nothing to save her Rennie fell heavily to the ground.

Fighting the blackness which threatened to engulf her, she heard the distant thud of hooves draw near and then a firm voice: 'Whoa, Lucifer—steady boy . . . steady . . .'

She struggled to rise, to show Todd that she could stand, that she was all right, but her body felt to be nailed to the ground. Through the mists of pain his face floated above her, taut and concerned. 'Lie still. You've had a bad fall.'

But she didn't want to give in to the dreadful nausea which assailed her, dragging her down, down into a whirlpool of dark red depths. Lila wouldn't have lain crumpled. Lila wouldn't . . . have . . . blacked . . . o . . . u . . . t.

There was a blur of light that danced and made weird patterns, brilliant at times, then indistinct. It was some minutes before Rennie realised that the bobbing image was the glow of a wallside lamp not far from where she lay. As her gaze righted itself she was able to slowly take stock of her surroundings—the long white bed she was tucked up in, the clothes locker across the room, the small armchair in the corner.

She became aware of the shadow beside her, a long white shape it seemed, bent over. It turned suddenly from the trolley with a starchy rustle and a kindly, gentle voice said, 'Ah, you're coming round. How do you feel?' The man in the white coat was tall and slender with sandy, slightly greying hair and a warm boyish smile which seemed out of place in his grave, lean face.

'I . . . don't know.' Rennie moved stiffly. 'Where am I?'

'This is the mine hospital. I'm Doctor Peter Dunbar.' As he continued to scribble smilingly on the pad beside him it all came back to Rennie.

'I . . . remember now.' She raised a hand to ease her aching head. 'Lucifer threw me. How long have I been here?'

'Two hours. Todd checked you over for broken bones, discovered you were still in one piece so he brought you in on his horse. He's outside.'

He turned to the door and Rennie struggled up to stop him. *No, not Todd now! Not to see her like this.* But the doctor, believing he was doing her a kindness, went out and spoke a few words. The next moment Todd stepped in.

He was still dressed as Rennie had last seen him, his white shirt streaked with earth. He looked weary, but his smile was at its usual teasing slant as he came towards the bed. 'So our tough engineer has been out for the count! I always knew that spanner-wielding approach was just a front.'

She couldn't speak for the lump in her throat. A tear escaped from beneath her lashes and trickled slowly down her cheek. His grin was lopsided as he stood beside her and asked with quizzical concern, 'Did I say something wrong, sweet Rennie what's-a-name?'

'No, of course not,' she swallowed. 'I'm all right.'

'You had us worried, but luckily it's nothing more than concussion.' Never had she been more aware of his vitality and strength as she was at this moment. 'Sleep now. You're in good hands. Peter's the best doctor we've got.' He smoothed the hair from her brow. 'Goodnight, young Rennie.'

'Goodnight, Todd.'

He went out and closed the door softly behind him and another tear slid down Rennie's cheek. He didn't know that she had wanted more than anything to be as competent as Lila in his eyes.

The sun was throwing copper rods of light on the wall when she awoke again. Later a Bantu orderly in spotless white cotton came to draw back the shutters from the windows with a wide smile, and afterwards placed a breakfast tray beside her. Bruised and stiff but otherwise feeling more or less herself again, she was able to sit propped up against the pillows sipping her coffee and contemplating the view.

There were strips of lawn outside the windows and flower beds and from this side of the mine compound, looking across the open veld, it was possible to see in the far distance the flat-topped range of the Jinju mountains, a misty gold now in the morning light, beyond which she was told were well-watered valleys and sub-tropical fruit-growing lands. Resting back, she mused for a while on how little she knew about the country of South Africa. All she had had time to think about since her arrival was her work. But she was aware and always had been of the savage splendour and the vastness, and the raw, primitive pulse of the land which beat just below the surface of its civilisation.

Mid-morning Doctor Dunbar looked in. In the daylight Rennie saw that he couldn't have been much older than Todd, but the gravity of his work had lined his face perhaps and given him a maturity beyond his years. He took her pulse and shone a little torch into her eyes and smiled with satisfaction at her progress. 'I think we can safely say that it was a straight case of concussion. But I'd rather you stayed here over the week-end just in case there are any bad headaches.'

Rennie grimaced. 'Stay in hospital like an invalid? But I feel perfectly well.'

'I know,' he nodded with an understanding light. 'But a knock on the head can sometimes have adverse effects. You were unconscious rather a long time and I'd prefer to keep you under observation for a couple of days.'

She consented with a heavy sigh and twinkling as he wrote out a prescription, he said, 'You can get up if you like. I'll send a boy over to your hut for some clothes. What about a pretty dress to brighten things up?'

'No, thanks,' she shook her head. 'I only wear jeans and tee-shirts.'

He crooked an eyebrow inquiringly at her over his rather

nice grey eyes. 'The only girl in the mine compound and you don't take advantage of the situation?'

'I'm an engineer,' she said flatly.

'I know,' he nodded, smiling. 'Todd told me. He seems to think that the job's too much for a girl. I'm afraid he's one of those old-fashioned types who believe that mining is a man's world.'

Rennie threw a look of disgust at the ceiling. 'He's been making that clear ever since I arrived,' she muttered.

There was humour in the doctor's gaze. 'I take it you two don't exactly hit it off?' He tore off the prescription slip and placed it on the bedside table.

'Like rock quartz on a grinding wheel,' she said drily.

Doctor Dunbar laughed. 'I'm sure you've yet to discover Todd's good side. Sceptical he might be on occasion, but if he's wrong he'll say so.'

'Mmmmm!' Rennie looked unconvinced, but it was impossible to be grim with the doctor's twinkling gaze on her, and seeing that he was in no hurry to leave she asked, not without curiosity, 'Do you run the hospital all by yourself?'

'I do have a little assistance,' he replied with amusement. 'Even though there are only sixty beds.'

'But accidents are rare, aren't they?' She hugged her knees. 'I mean, with all the precautions that are taken these days.'

'Yes, but sometimes we get heat sickness and fevers, and then there's always the malingerers, especially among the African boys who still believe in evil spells and witchcraft. Each case must be carefully checked out as a safeguard against epidemics.'

'Yes, I see what you mean.' Rennie's smile was all the wiser now. 'You keep busy.'

'I prefer to.' She thought he said it a little briskly as though he had a dread of finding time on his hands, although he softened this immediately with his playful gleam. 'I'm a doctor and I need patients to practise on.'

'Well, don't look at me,' she said laughingly. 'I'm only a week-end guest.' She liked Peter Dunbar. He was a gentle-natured person and yet there was a solid streak in him, a kind of warm dependability.

'You're quite safe.' His finely drawn mouth sloped into a grin and that was when he looked years younger. 'Actually I have another outlet for my surgical aspirations. I graft trees in my spare time.' He clipped his pen back into his top pocket and explained with his slim, expressive hands, 'A fruit tree will do all kinds of wonderful things if it's doctored properly. I'm trying to get some exotic types going in my garden. It's supposed to be practically impossible out here with the arid conditions, but I'm having a fair amount of success. Todd is giving me some useful advice.' He finished, smiling down at her, 'You must come and have a look round one day when you're mobile again.'

'I will. But I haven't the faintest idea which is your house,' she confessed.

'I'm at the end of C block, just across from the hospital.'

'Not the house with the rubber tree hedge and gorgeous blossom? I've often admired it,' she said glowingly, and then thoughtfully, 'but I thought that doctors had to take care of their hands. I mean, isn't tree grafting and dabbling with soil a hazard?'

'I wear gloves. I've grown quite used to working well clad and it's a way of passing the time out here.' Though he spoke lightly there was a look in his eyes which made her feel it was all part of his desperate measures to keep busy. Despite his quiet cordiality and gentle humour he had a kind of distinguished bearing and even to Rennie's young mind he seemed far too eminent a person to be stuck out in the wilds running a tiny mine hospital. But of course she didn't say so.

'Well, I must be getting on with my rounds,' he said cheerfully. 'I'll have a change of clothes sent over. You can sit out in the fresh air if you like, but don't go in the sun.'

After he had left Rennie explored the room barefoot. She winced occasionally at a wrenched muscle, but really she felt little the worse for her experience. Beside the window a glass door opened on to a little square of patio screened off from the next room by trelliswork and climbing greenery. After lunch, dressed in a pair of blue cotton slacks and white tee-shirt, a little paler perhaps, the lilac shadows more pronounced under her eyes, she sat out in an armchair and explored the view with her gaze. The air was warm about her bare arms and scented with the heavy green aroma of wild fig and bushveld willows, and philosophically she supposed there were worse ways to spend a Saturday afternoon.

Beyond the open gateway in the distance she could see a portion of the bowling green where several mine workers were enjoying a relaxing game. On a strip of lawn inside the hospital grounds two African inmates lounged on the grass. One wore a high-crowned canary-coloured straw hat and a brightly striped blanket swathed over his outdoor suit, though the heat of the sun must have been considerable. The other one, his balding head bare, his sandalled feet stuck out in front of him, leaned back on his hands, his huge straw hat beside him on the grass.

There were squat date palms in the grounds and rose hedges, and Rennie felt that there could now be no more surprises as to the well laid out order of the compound grounds. It could only have been a few short years ago that all this had been semi-desert and scrubland. Now there were trees and lawn and gardens, and there was no doubt that the outdoor amenities helped to make an all-round life for the isolated mine workers.

It was about four o'clock when Joshua the medical orderly came in to announce, 'The Miss has visitors. I'll bring tea.' He scuttled happily away before Rennie had time to ask questions and through the open door in walked Todd and Lila.

The latter was in a peach tailored trouser suit, her flame

hair swept back by a velvet headband revealing her exquisitely made up features; she waved a bundle of racing magazines. 'Todd insisted on bringing you flowers, but I told him you'd far rather have these.'

She tossed them down on the table beside Rennie and turned back to cast a clinical glance around the room. 'I hate these places. They seem to put a morbid brake on life and make one feel it's a sin to be healthy.'

'I hope these roses don't hear that,' Todd joked. 'I had them picked in their prime. How about a vase?'

'There's a tall glass in the bathroom which should do. They're lovely.' Rennie tried to appear lightheartedly unaffected by the visit. They had just breezed in and she too put on a breezy, careless air as though all afternoon callers were welcome.

The roses were arranged on the small dining table near the window, a scented cloud of lemon and pink blooms. 'All these rooms need is a touch of individuality,' Todd said, wiping his hands on his handkerchief.

'The girl's an engineer.' Lila viewed the floral arrangement with a touch of exasperated humour. 'Put a display of hydraulic components there and she'd be more likely to appreciate it.' She turned back to Rennie still sitting out on the little square of terrace. 'I flew in this morning and heard all about your disagreement with Lucifer. I'm afraid I drive him and brake him like mechanised transport. It's the only language he understands.'

'Maybe that was my trouble,' Rennie said wincingly. 'I rode him like a horse.'

'You rode him like a pony club competitor,' Todd put in with a grim smile. 'He'd have thrown you at the first ditch if there'd been one. And by the way,' he eyed her narrowly, 'While you were giving us all a scare last night refusing to come round I thought I might have to get in touch with your people. I discovered that your works record in the admin. block gave no indication of next of kin.'

'I haven't got round to filling them in yet,' Rennie said lightly.

'Rather a careless oversight, isn't it?'

'Oh, leave the girl alone, Todd,' Lila laughed with a passionless air of understanding. 'She's entitled to her little secrets like everyone else.'

Joshua appeared at that moment, much to Rennie's inward relief. On the tea tray there were delicately cut sandwiches, and the fluffy scones and pastries which the mine bakery excelled in. While her two visitors arranged the food and tea cups on the table trolley, Rennie tried to figure out what was different about Lila today. The sharp edge of her sardonic nature was not so noticeable. She had come to call and gave the appearance of being genuinely interested in the patient's welfare. Yet she was keyed up in some way. She had spent the time since arriving moving about the room; now she busied herself with unnecessary tasks at the table. Perhaps it was her phobia about hospitals which made her like this.

They were arranging the trolley on the terrace when Doctor Dunbar came in. 'Oh dear! I hope I'm not interrupting something.' He looked smilingly ill at ease at the guests, yet Rennie was sure this wasn't the hour for taking temperatures.

Todd, draped against the trelliswork, cup in hand, said lazily, 'Give the bedside manner a rest, Peter, and come and join us in a break.'

The doctor put the thermometer back in its case. 'Well, I suppose I can spare a little time. Van der Merwe is resting after his tonsillectomy and Zebbe Gugushe has never left his chair since he was brought in. And as our young horse rider here appears to be on the mend,' he smiled at Rennie, 'there are no urgent cases.'

'I heard about young Zebb.' Todd poured a cup of tea and handed it to the doctor. 'If he believes he's got the evil eye on him what can you do?'

'Not a great deal, I'm afraid, but I'm obliged to try. If Zebb has made up his mind to die nothing will stop him.' The doctor took a sip of his tea, then looked at the other guests. 'Hello, Lila.'

Resting against the rails that separated the tiny outdoor space from the flower beds, Lila didn't return the greeting. Instead she commented with waspish amusement, 'Still concerning yourself with the small problems of a mining community, Peter? I've yet to discover what you find attractive about this backwater.'

'The peace, for one thing,' the doctor said lightly, though he didn't sound very convincing. 'I was brought up in wild, untamed country. I prefer it to skyscraper blocks and city noise.'

'Do you?' Lila tilted a disbelieving eyebrow. 'When you know you could command ten times the fee and respect in a Johannesburg hospital?'

'The patients are the same wherever one works, my dear,' Peter said with his sad smile.

'Is it true that this man Zebb is convinced he's going to die?' Rennie asked, getting back to the evil eye subject.

'If we don't discover who's behind the mischief I'm afraid he will just literally waste away,' Peter Dunbar nodded.

'I saw a case like it in Kenya once.' Todd eased his weight against the trellis. 'A young Masai was discharged from the hospital as incurable. The missionaries in his village did everything they could, but he lay on his bed and became a living skeleton. Then it was discovered he had married a girl previously betrothed to someone else. The chief of the village was threatened unless he named the culprit and within a few days the Masai was taking broth and learning how to walk again.'

The doctor nodded. 'I've no doubt one of the boys has a grudge against Zebb.' He sighed. 'They work with scientific machinery and advanced techniques, yet the old ways still cling. Black Magic ... witchcraft ... and there's no modern medicine that will help.'

They chatted on desultorily about the case, later switching to other topics of conversation as the sandwiches dwindled. Lila poured the second cups of tea and handed round the pastries. She talked normally with the two men, even ribbing the doctor occasionally in a bright, metallic way. There was no sign of that earlier show of nerves, but once or twice as she bent over the trolley Rennie noticed the slight trembling of her hands.

Around five Todd made a move to leave. 'Time to get going,' he said, placing down his cup and saucer. 'We mustn't tire the patient.'

'Nonsense,' Rennie said shyly. 'I'm perfectly fit.' Throughout their stay she had tried not to notice Todd, looking bronzed and virile in fawn tropical suit and shirt, but now as his green gaze rested on her she knew she had been far more aware of his presence than was good for her. His look was humorously probing as he drawled, 'You still look pale to me. Take care of her, Peter. As the only girl engineer this side of the Limpopo river she carries a certain amount of prestige.'

'Don't worry,' the doctor twinkled at Rennie. 'I think we're going to find she's got a tough shell beneath that fragile, feminine exterior.' He turned to Lila, making ready to go. 'Will you be staying in Vukasi long?' he asked pleasantly.

'Over the week-end, I expect,' she replied offhandedly. And then with a touch of her earlier smiling acid, 'Why?'

'Just that you ought to take more care speeding up and down the country roads,' came the even reply.

'I flew in,' she tossed her russet locks.

'That's just as bad. You're twice as reckless in a plane.' The doctor's grave eyes didn't quite meet hers. 'I should try and tone it down a bit, my dear, when you're making these trips.'

'Why? Are you hoping you won't have to pick up the

pieces?' If Lila saw the look of pain which passed fleetingly across Doctor Dunbar's face she gave no sign of it.

Waiting in the open doorway, Todd looked at his watch. 'If we're going to have dinner in Tombaza we'll have to get moving. It's quite a drive. So long, Peter.' He gave Rennie a nod of farewell, and with a smiling, 'Goodbye, you two,' Lila preceded him out.

Joshua spent some time clearing away the remnants of the afternoon tea, and while he worked Doctor Dunbar stood gazing out into the distance from the little terrace, lost in thought. When the medical orderly had departed Rennie asked as a point of conversation, 'Have you known Lila long?'

'For quite a number of years,' the doctor nodded with a faraway look.

'You're fond of her, aren't you?' Rennie said with a gentle gleam.

His smile crooked, he brought his mind back to the matters in hand. 'Does it show?'

'Only to an outsider like me,' Rennie joked, trying to make light of the whole thing.

He didn't elaborate on the subject. He was long overdue on his rounds and after looking her over with his professional eye and taking her pulse he left her in his usual cheerful vein. 'Early to bed, don't forget. And tomorrow we'll probably be giving you a discharge.'

Left alone, Rennie found her own gaze wandering out across the vast grasslands to the low-lying mountains. She sat until the sunset made a splash of fiery gold behind their black peaks and the sky strewn with violet clouds changed from turquoise to the electric blue of night. And through it all the same thoughts circled round in her mind. Doctor Dunbar was in love with Lila, and Lila wanted Todd as much as she could want anything that wasn't metal and speed. But what about Todd? Was he in love with Lila too? He had taken her out to dinner and right now they would be sitting under the same African sky, mellow and lit with stars.

Rennie rose stiffly at last and made her way indoors. Perhaps it was the after effects of her bump on the head, but she felt low-spirited and miserable.

CHAPTER SEVEN

DUSK was softening the sprawling mine complex the following evening when Rennie left the hospital. She was making her uncertain way outdoors after leaving Doctor Dunbar's office when she saw a familiar figure pushing a tea trolley along the opposite corridor fronting the main entrance. The slim, boyish frame was clad in hospital white, and that neat head of glossy chestnut red hair she would recognise anywhere. 'Darrell!' She couldn't help but stare. 'What on earth are you doing here?'

'Hi!' He gave her a wave as he approached. Then dumping the trolley to one side, he said, 'That's everybody attended to, so I can knock off for a while.' And looking at her with a speculative grin, 'If you're not doing anything special we could go and have a drink.'

'I'm in no hurry.' She spoke truthfully, for there was only the solitary bachelor bungalow awaiting her.

Darell led her along the corridor and through a door into an open courtyard surrounded by a shady veranda on top of which was a cinema projection room and an opposite wall-side screen for the benefit of convalescing patients. He found somewhere to sit among the colourful chairs and tables and disappearing for a moment returned with two glasses of orange juice.

Astride a chair he threw a mouthful back, swigged it round so that his youthful adam's apple flew up and down and said with a look at the tiny projection room, 'I've seen a couple of good films here. *The Four Feathers*—incredibly dated but worth watching, and *King Solomon's Mines*—not bad if you like Stewart Granger. The Africans like to see films about their own country. They couldn't care less when they were made.' His grin was prominent again. 'And I get a free show too. There's always someone with a septic toe or a lacerated foot who needs pushing around.'

All this time Rennie had not ceased to view him with wonder. She said at last with a puzzled laugh, 'I don't get all this, Darrell. Do you mean to say you work here?'

'I do my best.' Some of his old diffidence showed as he took another gulp of his drink.

'But surely it's too much for you on top of your job in the mining complex?' She spoke with girlish concern.

'I don't just come here weekends,' he hastened to correct her. 'I'm a full-blown medical orderly—well, trainee, that is.'

Rennie couldn't drag her gaze from him. She saw the healthy pink colour of his skin, his clinical white suit, the jacket of which, with its round neck buttoning down one side of his chest, flattered him no end. He had a clearness of the eye, a kind of below-the-surface zest which was new to her. She said, not without humour, casting her mind back, 'The last time I saw you, you were having trouble with a new desk outside the administration block. That's ages ago, isn't it?'

He nodded with a rueful smile. 'I seemed to make a mess of everything I touched. If they wanted a bungler they just sent for Timpson. I was even having serious thoughts of giving up the idea of South Africa for a new life, kin or no kin.'

'But you obviously didn't.' Rennie took a sip of her orange juice.

He shook his head, dreaming a little. 'It's funny how you don't know yourself. All my life I've been aiming at the wrong things and wondering why I made such a muck of them.' He came back to her. 'Oh, I was ready to quit all right, put in my notice and everything. I remember that night Todd Dillman asked me over to his house for a drink. The old man was still away then. We had a long talk, almost an argument. I told him I was finished, but he insisted on getting to the bottom of what I really wanted to do. We went through everything, but there seemed nothing. I think he dragged out of me what I didn't know myself, that industry and commercialism left me cold.' Darrell hesitated, decided to go on, and gave her a shy, embarrassed look. 'You're going to laugh a this, but when we broke it down I discovered that more than anything I wanted to help people.'

'Why should I laugh?' Rennie spoke in genuine tones. 'There are thousands of people who feel like you do. Social workers . . . doctors . . .' She thought of Peter Dunbar.

'That's what Todd said. It was he who suggested the hospital. I thought it was a mad idea at first, but I'm growing to like it. There's something . . . well, I don't know . . .' he scratched his head shyly perplexed again, 'rewarding, I suppose you'd call it, about doing things for those who can't do for themselves.'

'And yet I was laid up in there,' she teased, 'and you never came to say hello.'

'I wanted to,' his brow wrinkled with boyish concern, 'but you were one of the doctor's special cases and I'm only a novice, remember.'

'I'll let you off,' she laughed. 'But if I ever have to repeat the experience—heaven forbid!—I shall insist on having you to wait on me.'

Darrell grinned in agreement and she drank to his new self-assurance. He had got a foothold, tentative though it was, in his adopted country, and she was happy for him.

They chatted until it was time for Darrell to go back on duty, then Rennie left. As she walked along the lamplit road to her bungalow, the sky that translucent jade before dark, she was thoughtful. So Todd had gone out of his way to put

Darrell straight. And it must have been soon after their somewhat heated discussion at his house that first Saturday afternoon. She remembered, she had taken Darrell's side.

She tugged at a leaf in passing. What a strange and irritating man he was! Always showing understanding and compassion where she least expected it, then dousing down the gnawing ache in her. But she mustn't think of Todd, musn't allow herself to recall the hard, laconic charm of him. These last few days she had been perilously near to giving rein to her feelings, but that was all finished now. She was an engineer at the Kramer diamond mine, and that and that alone must remain the only important thing to her.

She tried to brisk up her step and take an interest in her surroundings. Over in the middle distance she could see the bright lights of the community centre, and at the far end of the adjoining block the library and reading rooms. On her left a line of sentinel gums bordered the edge of the compound and above them the first pearl-like stars were beginning to appear. But her steps dragged when she turned the corner and made her way along the last deserted stretch of road. At the end lay her small habitation, a bleak and lonely outpost. But no bleaker than the thought of the life ahead to which she had dedicated herself.

Monday morning came and with it the roaring, clattering activity at the mine face. Rennie went to work as usual slightly stunned at the sluggish, weak feeling which persisted all over her. Sitting in her chair in her room at the hospital, doing small chores around the bungalow last night, she had felt reasonably well. But as she swung about now from one taxing job to another, the whole sorry escapade of her riding accident caught up with her. Her legs trembled alarmingly and she went from hot sweats to cold ones with the perspiration drying like ice on her skin.

Of course she knew it was simply reaction. A couple of days and it would all have passed. It was clearly a question of having to toughen up again. She kept out of the way of the others as much as possible so that no one would see her strained, washed out look. Somehow she managed to get through the morning.

She was tightening up the last screw in a faulty crane shaft when a pale blue Landrover trundled over the uneven ground and came to a stop some distance away beside the site office. There was a fresh flurry of activity among the mine workers and it was obvious that the mine owner was not in the habit of putting in appearances at the quarry face.

His step a little uncertain as always, he picked his way over the rocky ground, squinting here and there at any man who wasn't putting his back into his job, having a clipped word with the ones in authority. Rennie thought she might avoid him, but he was heading her way and she had a feeling he had been making for her all along, though he was too foxy to let her know it.

He stopped beside her and boldly watched her at work, and to her annoyance her hand trembled on the heavy nut she was adjusting. 'I came to see that you're justifying the wages I'm paying you.' There was no beating about the bush with Coulton Kramer, she thought, gritting her teeth.

'I think you'll find you're getting value for money,' she replied icily.

His frosty blue eyes were piercingly observant beneath the shaggy overhang of his white brows. 'Todd told me you took a tumble,' he said with a slightly malicious smirk.

'I fell off a horse,' Rennie made the statement flatly. Would no one let her forget her blunder! 'But I'm all right now.'

'You look like death.' He eyed her mercilessly. 'What you need is a few good steak meals.'

'It's true I haven't had time to get into my stride again yet,' she admitted haughtily. 'But I can assure you my work won't suffer.'

He waved away her reply and asked, 'What time's your

lunch break? Aaron's making a casserole today.'

'I don't knock off until one-thirty and I always eat a packed lunch,' she replied primly.

'It's almost that now.' His frosty gaze heated up to a fiery glare as he watched her calmly carrying on with her job and rasped, 'You may be an engineer, young lady, but I'm the boss round here, so drop your things and make it snappy.'

Rennie knew she had better do as she was told. Besides, she was in no mood to do battle today with the irascible mine owner. Her head throbbed and the idea or relieving herself of her heavy tools for a while was too tempting to resist.

She followed him to the car where he said, jabbing a finger at the wheel, 'You can drive me home. I hate steering myself. Got past it a long time ago.'

Rennie got into the driving seat with a curled smile. Though she was supposed to be the guest he was determined to make use of her as he probably did everyone at the mine. She drove unhurriedly along the three-mile stretch from the quarry face and later the wide avenues of the residential compound, and he sat beside her, his jaw thrust forward and his eagle eye viewing his terrain.

When she drew up inside the grounds of the mine owner's secluded property a servant in white jacket and black trousers—possibly this was Aaron—stood on the steps of the house looking nervous. 'Master, the meal is cooked. All is ready to serve and you are not here ... I fear that ...'

'I'm coming! I'm coming!' Coulton Kramer stumped up the steps. 'Can't a man turn his back a minute?' He indicated Rennie with a thrust of his chin. 'Set a place for this girl here. She's eating with us today.'

They went through the spacious living room to an adjoining dining room where an oval table was laid with a white cloth and napkins and plain cutlery and glassware, and the curtainless windows showed views of the walled-in grounds. Aaron came through the swing door with a fresh supply of cutlery and linen. 'There's a tap in the kitchen if you want to wash your hands,' Rennie was told abruptly, and by the time she returned the steaming food was on the table and her sickly appetite was picking up at the savoury aromas coming from the dishes.

It was a long time since she had dined in so civilised a manner and despite her cool resentment towards the mine owner she ate shyly and with no little strain. Coulton Kramer, fond of his food, paid no attention to her stiff attitude. He filled his own glass and hers with a good South African wine and kept them topped up throughout the meal. There had to come a time when the ice broke between them and conversation began to flow, albeit a little stiltedly.

It was after the servant had left them to return to other duties in the kitchen. Rennie had been watching him with interest at the table. He was different somehow from the other Africans she had seen at the mine. Tall and thin as a reed, he had big hands, a finely shaped head, no longer youthful, and a soft tread. 'Aaron's an Ovambo,' the mine owner said when he had gone. 'Doesn't belong to this part of the world. He's been with me since my mining days in South West Africa. And come to think of it,' he fixed her with his steely blue eye over the top of his knife and fork, 'you don't belong to this part of the world either. How come you've never filled in that kind of information on your works records?'

Todd again! She tightened her lips. When she didn't reply her host thrust out his chin and probed doggedly, 'What part of the old country do you come from, anyway?'

'It wouldn't interest you,' she brushed off his curiosity in even tones. 'You're not English, and you're not South African.'

'Oh, you've noticed that, have you!' he said in his accusing way. And dabbing at a trickle of gravy on his chin,

'Well, just in case you're wondering, I'm a Canadian by birth. Got my Ph.D. at McGill University in 1938 and the next year came out to Rhodesia to work for a mining company.'

Content enough to have turned the attention from herself, Rennie listened with a polite ear.

'Knocked around Africa as a geologist for quite a while. Did a spell at Oranjemund and spent some years in the goldfields at Witwatersrand. But diamonds have always had a fascination for me, and I figured I had a pretty good idea where they could be found. It wasn't easy and it took a long time. Now look at me!' He prodded a fork at her to give force to his words. 'Governor and sole director of Kramer Diamonds Ltd.'

Rennie took a sip of wine as though only mildly impressed.

His fork found its way to the table. His eagle eye had softened and he was saying as though in a daydream, 'Have you ever seen a pile of diamonds washed and gleaming on the sorting blotter? Pale blues, there are, and goldy ones, and ice white and some like mercury.' There was a look in his eye, not of greed but of pride.

'Among the quarry chippings they look like bits of frosted glass.' Rennie helped herself to fruit.

'They do,' he agreed with her with alacrity. 'But when they're cut—ah, when they're cut! The transition from rough stone to shimmering diamond is a unique metamorphosis, uniting the pure strength of nature with the adeptness of the human mind and hand.'

'You're almost poetical about them,' Rennie ventured boldly. 'I wonder you don't sport them yourself. A diamond tiepin, or cufflinks or something.'

'What for?' He glared at her. 'I found 'em, didn't I? Isn't that enough?'

Aaron brought in coffee and after it Rennie sat back, strengthened by the food.

— — — — — — CUT-OFF ALONG HERE — — — — — —

Postage will
be paid by
Mills & Boon
Limited

Do not affix postage stamps if posted in
Gt. Britain, Channel Islands or N. Ireland.

BUSINESS REPLY SERVICE
Licence No. CN.81

MILLS & BOON READER SERVICE,
P.O. Box No. 236
14 Sanderstead Road,
SOUTH CROYDON,
SURREY, CR2 9PU.

2

'That's better,' the mine owner snapped. 'Got some colour in your cheeks at last. Been living on sandwiches and cold snacks, I bet.'

She didn't reply to this, partly because it was true, and partly because she refused to jump to attention each time he barked at her. When at length he rose after the meal she followed him out. But he didn't go back to the living room as she had expected. Instead he took her along a carpeted corridor and into another room. There was nothing in here but tables and every one was piled high with reading matter.

'Take a look at those,' he said in his abrupt fashion. 'First editions, all of them. Know anything about books?'

Rennie hadn't waited to be asked. Fingering a superb velvet binding lovingly and flicking through the copper-plate contents, she said, 'I know that such treasures shouldn't be left lying around.'

'Well, I know that,' he said testily. 'But what do we do? The floor's the only place left to stack 'em.'

Rennie turned frigid at his tones. 'Obviously you need someone to classify the subjects in alphabetical order,' she said woodenly. 'And the same with the authors' names, I would think.'

'Makes sense,' he nodded, viewing the muddle. He looked at her, she thought a little slyly, and rapped, 'And since you're the only one who's come up with the bright idea, you've got the job.'

'Me?' She took a step back. 'But I've never had anything to do with books. And besides, I've got to get back to work.'

'Work!' he jeered, looking her up and down. 'Ha! One puff of wind and you'll blow over. You're on light duties for the next few days, and that's an order.'

Rennie set her lips. Pulling herself up, she said thinly, 'You may own the diamond mine, Mr Kramer, but you don't own me. Thank you for the lunch.'

The problem was finding the way out. First the carpeted corridor, the stumping steps behind her, then the dining room, heavy breathing at her shoulder, and from here ...
'Doggone it, girl, I *want* you to stay.'

Rennie slackened her steps halfway across the living room. She recalled that the mine owner had gone out of his way to call on her at the quarry site. But she was too mixed up to know whether he had brought her back to his house for his own ends or out of a shrewd, fatherly concern. And did it matter? Leith had leaned on her rather a lot of late. What if she in turn took things easy? No harm would come of him having to do his fair share of the work for a while. She was weakening. In her peaky condition the thought of not having to tug around with noisy machinery at the mine face for a few days was bliss. Besides—her hand slid along the fabric of an armchair—this house with its spacious rooms and neat furnishings reminded her of home. What would be more uplifting than to spend a little time here?

As though her decision came hard she turned and waited several seconds before speaking. 'I'll need a sheet of paper or something ...'

'I can get you that. As much as you like.' The mine owner's eyes leapt but he was too wily to openly demonstrate his delight. However, his step was light as he followed her back to the library. He clearly intended to pitch in, for he not only supplied the paper, but put himself at the ready for handing her the books, though his countenance remained scowling to make up for his earlier loss of face in asking her to stay.

'We'll have to take them one at a time.' Pen in hand, Rennie was cool and practical. 'Title on the left, author's name on the right. Better make an inventory first of all the works you possess.'

For the next hour or so all kinds of wondrous material passed through her hands; faded leather-bound works by Shakespeare and Shelley. Dust-ingrained volumes by

Burns, Dumas, Flaubert and Calderon. And spanking new first editions by contemporary writers of the day. She was starting on her second sheet of paper when the mine owner, who had the job of re-depositing the books when they were finished with, exclaimed tetchily, 'This is no good! They're all getting mixed up again. I can't remember now which we've done.'

Rennie drew in a breath and pointed out with patient detachment, 'It will always be a muddle until you get some bookshelves. And you really need a cabinet for your file index.'

'Now where am I going to get those kind of things out here?' he queried pettishly.

Rennie shrugged. 'There's probably a local supplier. Wykveld isn't that hopeless. I've seen a couple of stores myself where they might stock these items.'

'I never go into town.' Impatiently he brushed aside the idea. 'Haven't been there in years.'

'Maybe that's why you're so crusty.' The slender thread of her self-control finally snapped. 'You live with your books and forget there's a real world outside.'

There was a sizzling silence. Though she felt no regret at having spoken her mind, Rennie was a little concerned as to the effect of her words, and afraid that the mine owner might have apoplexy, she offered a suggestion, 'We could clear off one of the tables completely and put only the listed books there.'

He scowled at her from beneath the shaggy overhang of his eyebrows and snorted and grumbled as they went to work, but he made no comment on her scathing remark.

The cook boy brought in refreshments from time to time and by the end of the day a small start had been made on the colossal task. The grounds were bathed in soft evening light when Rennie got ready to leave. On the steps out front Coulton Kramer told her, 'Aaron will drive you back. See you in the morning, nine o'clock sharp. I'll let the office know you won't be in to work for a few days.'

She sat beside the gentle Ovambo in the luxurious Land-rover and waved him a friendly goodbye after he had dropped her off outside her bungalow.

The following day she used her little range truck to get to Mr Kramer's house. When she arrived he was in the dining room, a boiled egg on his plate and coffee pot nearby. He took one look at the doorway and fired at her, 'Had breakfast? Sit down. I've told Aaron to bring tea. That's what the English always drink, isn't it?'

His eyes had their usual keen brilliance, but she thought she detected a mingling of humour and sheepishness there.

She pulled out a chair at the side of the table and said, allowing her own face to crack slightly into a smile, 'We're fond of tea, but like you Canadians and your coffee we don't drink it all the time.'

As she hadn't actually bothered with any breakfast, and she had a feeling that the mine owner was shrewd enough to have guessed it, she ate, surprised at her own appetite and at the rejuvenating qualities in two cups of piping hot tea.

Afterwards they transferred to the library, but they hadn't been working more than half an hour when Coulton Kramer, rubbing his chin agitatedly as though wondering how to broach the subject, suddenly blurted, 'This store in town you were talking about. Reckon they'll stock book-shelves and the like?'

'I'm sure of it.' Rennie ran her finger down the list in her hand and ticked off another title.

He seemed impatient with her indifference and snapped, 'Well, why don't we go there now? You know more about these sort of things than I do, and you handle the Land-rover pretty well.'

Rennie raised her gaze slowly and he turned his away hastily, but as she looked at the back of him her own began to twinkle deeply. She was beginning to think he was an old fraud, using his irascibility as a cloak to hide his loneliness. She said brightly and in softer tones, 'Sounds like a good idea. We'll measure up first and then you can decide if you want to make use of all the wall space.'

Later, at the wheel of the Landrover, she noticed the expressions of surprise at the main gates of the mine compound when it was seen that Coulton Kramer was actually taking a drive. Everyone sprang to attention and of course there was no such thing as stopping the mine owner's car for a search. Out on the road, the latter sat hunched in his seat reluctantly, or so it seemed, watching the view. Rennie thought that if he practically never left the mine much of this would be new to him, the Vukasi roadside store, the straw huts of the village through the trees at the riverside, the farm fields and buildings. But he startled her by pointing out the Dutch-style manor. 'Rosedale.' His glance was glued to it as they drove by. 'I went there once. Todd is doing a good job planting all those trees—if you like that sort of thing.'

Rennie looked at him. 'Don't you?' she asked with a half smile. 'I think it must be wonderful to live in a house tucked away among gorgeous trees and greenery with the sound of tinkling water coming in through the open windows.'

'Oh, you do!' He said it as a sneer, then eyed her with an underhand glance which was shrewd and wickedly inquiring. 'What makes you think I'd like that kind of thing?'

Rennie shrugged. 'The grounds where you are now are very stark. You could afford it,' she said simply.

'Humph.' With this somewhat inarticulate reply he took to the view again.

The Landrover, expensively fitted out with every modern device which the mine owner probably never used, ate up the miles. By mid-morning they were browsing around the furniture store on the corner of a shady avenue not far from the Wykveld hotel. Rennie was pleasantly surprised at the quantity of goods for sale and the warehouse proportions of the store in a building at the rear.

The demand for bookshelves was disappointing. Though they hunted around they could find only two tall narrow pieces, hopelessly out of dimension for the library space which needed to be filled. But Rennie had an idea. 'I've been thinking, Mr Kramer——'

'Shsh ... don't call me that here,' he hushed her sharply, though there was no assistant within earshot. And quickly devoting his scowling attention to a set of occasional tables in carved teak, he muttered, 'Coult's good enough when we're out.'

'Sorry ... Coult,' she smiled. And viewing the oddments around them, 'Much of their stock seems to be produced on the premises, so it's possible that they'll make the book-shelves to your own requirements. We could give them the measurements and ask them to deliver when they're ready.'

'Well, what are we waiting for?' He waved her ahead of him to the chief salesman, a tubby-figured African in gay shirt and city-tailored trousers.

There was no problem and within a few minutes it was all arranged. On the strength of this the mine owner shunted Rennie towards the office section. After talking it over they bought a desk and a couple of swivel chairs and a filing cabinet for under the window in the library.

Outdoors again the sun struck them with its full African force as they crossed the street. Rennie felt the beads of perspiration forming on her upper lip. Though she was stronger on her feet since her fall from the horse she still got these bouts of weakness and sometimes her head throb-bed hollowly.

She didn't think she stumbled, but when they got to the Landrover Coult Kramer said, shooting her a look, 'If you think you're humping me back in this heat you're mis-taken. Isn't there a place round here where a man can slake his thirst?'

'At the hotel there's a pretty garden, nice and shady.'
She bit back her smile. She knew better than to show a hint
of gratitude.

It was pleasant and restful sitting beneath a kokerboom
tree sipping iced limes. Rennie was just about on nodding
terms with the staff at the hotel, but no one had any idea
who her elderly gentleman companion was, nor did they
show any curiosity. When, in due course, the pair departed
an average tip was found on the table.

It was well after midday when they got back to the mine.
Rennie drove into the grounds of the sprawling house on
the veld and they thankfully trudged in to the cool of the
indoors. After lunch Coult snoozed in his chair on the
veranda and Rennie, feeling equally idle, flicked through the
pages of a magazine and listened to the lazy sound of
insects droning on the still air and the distant hum of
activity in the mine compound.

At four o'clock they made a start in the library and
worked until seven. Coult said, as Rennie stacked the books
recently listed, 'You'd better stay to dinner. No sense in
your going back to your place to cook yourself a meal when
we've got Aaron.'

So she sat opposite Coult at the oval table while the lilac
shadows of dusk stole around the house and the lights of
the dining room cast a cosy glow. The food was good and
the cluttered library faded from their thoughts. They were
well satisfied with the start that had been made.

Bookshelves are simple to make and on Thursday the
desk and everything they had ordered at the Wykveld stores
was delivered. Enlisting the help of the houseboy, on his
knees waxing the living room floor, and Romaano, watering
the shrubbery in the garden—Aaron in his smart white
butler jacket stirring his potions in the kitchen was a little
above shifting furniture—they managed to get everything in
place.

After lunch, though the library had been transformed and

there was somewhere to put everything, Coult showed a disinclination for work. He fidgeted with a book with a mischievous expression on his face, then putting it back on the desk he said suddenly, 'Let's go out.'

Rennie told him humorously, 'You're a recluse, remember.'

He eyed her with a subtle gleam and wagged a finger at her accusingly. '*Now* who wants to stay with the books all the time?'

She put down her pen and title list and asked laughingly, 'Where do you suggest?'

He was thoughtful. 'Ever seen any wild game while you've been in Africa?'

'About the most I can lay claim to,' Rennie smiled ruefully, 'is a couple of duikers we passed on the road once. I thought one had to go quite a way from here to see anything really worthwhile?'

'I know a place,' he led the way to the door. 'Used to go there years ago and as far as I know nothing's changed.'

There was refrigerated drinking water in the Landrover and a stocked hamper should they get hungry, and together with the air-conditioning, deep upholstery and tinted glass, driving for Rennie was a pleasure. Out of the mine gates they left the road once they had passed the settlement and Coult directed her towards a track barely visible which struck off into open country.

She saw after a while that they were making for the sandstone bluffs, rust red now and purple shadow against the hot blue sky, and she recalled that Darrell had mentioned that there was wild game out there. But he was wrong about it being an open plain. Beyond the bluffs was a tremendous space bordered closely by similar sandstone ranges. It was like a huge amphitheatre and the tall yellowing grass and tangled trees throbbed and crackled in the heat and the stillness of the interior.

They drove in between towering buttresses no more than

a hundred yards apart at the base and Coult told her, 'There's only one other entrance over to the north-east. The animals herd in from that direction looking for water in the dry season. The place is littered with rock pools. They stay and breed and move on if the mood takes them. A lot drift this way and spread out towards the Limpopo going south.'

Rennie looked at the vast enclosed space the jagged outline of its parallel ranges like a fortress against the milky glare of the sky. 'It's fantastic!' she breathed.

'They call it the Aasvogel Arena—that's Afrikaans for vulture—Every year when the place is bursting at the seams licenses are given and you can take your pick of wild game.'

'How awful!' She turned in her seat. 'It's like a trap.'

'Maybe,' the mine owner nodded. 'And then again it might be that nature likes to give a great big helping hand once in a while.' At Rennie's puzzled look he explained with a harsh chuckle, 'These are not the tabby cat pets and harmless balls of fur you drool over in England. A leopard can cause a lot of trouble in a village or an outlying district. They have been known to steal up to a veranda in the dark and take a sleeping dog from its chair, and a baby tucked up in its cot in its own room is no safer. And did you know that an elephant can do more damage underfoot in an hour than a couple of tractors?' He shrugged. 'Just like they keep the pests down in your country—squirrels, for instance, when they damage the trees—so we thin out the species every now and again when they become too numerous.'

'Putting it like that,' Rennie nodded soberly, 'I suppose you've got a point.'

'You'll find a rough track to the left of those fever trees, if I'm not mistaken,' Coult pointed. 'Take it slow and we'll see what turns up.'

Rennie drove into the quivering stillness uncertainly. Here she could feel the naked pulse of Africa in the waving feathery grass, in the creeper-festooned trees and the bushes thrusting up clusters of blood-red flowers. Her nervousness must have been apparent, for Coult reassured her with a smile, 'We're quite safe. Nothing can hurt us in the truck.'

Rennie wasn't so sure. He had spoken of leopard and elephant. What would she do if she were to look straight into the blazing amber eyes of the forest cat, or drive head-on into the path of a towering, tusked creature!

As it happened they saw nothing of either species during the afternoon. But if this was a disappointment—privately Rennie knew only relief—there was much more to compensate. Like the pair of sable antelopes, ridged-horned and magnificent, grazing on an open stretch, and a group of young giraffes with soft, dewy eyes standing in the mottled shade of thorn trees. Parked by a dry watercourse they saw a troop of impala with white-banded hind legs, the glossy-coated ewes mothering their lambs. And the high spot of the visit, for Rennie at least, was the sight of a family of white-collared monkeys swinging low above the Landrover on their way to a grove of wild fig trees.

Bird calls and weird sounds of evening were starting up when they drove out between the towering sandstone bluffs and back to Vukasi and the mine compound. Aaron, as always on edge when food was waiting to be served, sighed with relief when he saw the Landrover turn into the grounds. Because of the unusual heat and the fact that he was paid to use his head, he had set a table among the cool greenery on the veranda, and it was here that Rennie and the mine owner whiled away the evening discussing the events of the afternoon.

It was Friday morning, the day after, when Todd showed up at the house. They had made a leisurely start after breakfast in the library and had got several blocks of books in alphabetical order around the shelves. Rennie was writing up information on an index card near the window and paid no attention to the footsteps that came in through the library door until she heard the mine owner exclaim with a chuckle,

'Well, if it isn't the feller with the green fingers! Getting them trees in, are you, Todd!'

'Morning, Coult. How's the mining business?'

Her heart thudding at the lazy greeting, Rennie took her time in looking up.

The mine owner, in a world far removed from the diamond digging scene, replied with piquant humour, 'Ask my accountants.'

She brought her glance round casually to meet Todd's then. He was in shirt sleeves, rolled up to show powerful biceps, and work trousers. His gaze on her, he said, 'Tried the engineers's office a couple of times through the week. Buttonholed Leith this morning. He told me you'd been off sick.'

'An exaggeration,' she replied lightly, avoiding his searching look. 'I was simply relegated to other duties for a while.'

He thrust his hands into his pockets and surveying the library with its additional furnishings and the piles of books with interest, he asked, 'What gives?'

'Everything, my boy!' Coult chortled. 'I finally got on to doing something about this blamed clutter as you've been dogging me to.' His gleam on Rennie was roguish and a little ashamed. 'I took advantage of the fact that our second engineer happens to be a girl who doesn't hit it off with horses and we've got on like a house on fire.'

Idly mocking as always, Todd was noticing for himself the change in Rennie; the soft golden bloom on her cheeks which contrasted favourably with the apple green of her tee-shirt, the delphinium blue of her eyes, clear and rested now and faintly sparkling within their fringe of dark lashes. He drawled without moving his gaze, 'Maybe you've done her a favour, Coult. She looks better as a librarian than she does as an engineer.'

'That's only because you're prejudiced,' she said briskly. 'Naturally I'll help Coult with the books all I can in my spare time, but on Monday morning I'll be back at the quarry site as usual.'

Todd's smile became part sneer. 'You really carry a torch for this job of yours, don't you?'

The weariness stirred inside her, together with the tightness at his satirical tones. If only he knew! She'd give it up tomorrow, but the choice wasn't hers. She replied smoothly enough, 'You make it appear so, but I'm simply a girl trying to get ahead in her profession.'

'Even if it kills you.'

'It's no good trying to change her, Todd,' the mine owner put in. 'I tried. You'll stay to lunch now you're here?'

'No thanks,' Todd declined somewhat tautly, and dividing his attention between the two of them. 'I dropped in to check up on local gossip. I heard that you drove out to the Aasvogel Arena yesterday.'

'The devil you did!' The mine owner's eyebrows shot up, not amused. 'Who's been talking?'

'Don't ask me,' Todd shrugged. 'Practically the whole of the hill settlement must have seen your Landrover cutting across the veld towards the bluffs.' He looked a little grim. 'I'm surprised at your choice of picnic spot, Coult. You know as well as I do that the wild game out there can be pretty dangerous. It's not the place for . . .' he searched for the right words rather more gently.

'For a sick old man and a defenceless girl. That's what you were going to say, weren't you!' The mine owner gleamed, not one whit put out.

'There's nothing sick about you, Coult,' Todd said with a smile. 'You're as tough as an old boot and you know it.' His motives for leaving Rennie out of it were patently obvious.

'You bet I am,' Coult retorted. 'And I'll tell you something else. That Landrover's built like a tank. A rogue elephant would have a hard time denting it, and I knew that when we went out there. I'm not feeble-minded yet, Todd.'

'Okay,' this brought a grin. 'But next time you feel like

driving out that way let me know and I'll lend you one of my boys. That a deal?'

'If it'll make you feel better, it's a deal,' the older man consented good-naturedly.

'Good! Now I'd better be on my way.' Todd made his farewells, then stopped to run his eye over Rennie. 'Pity about the hair,' he said with the old quizzical expression.

She knew that he was picturing it under her cap when she was back at the quarry face, and hinting that it ought to stay as it was, loosely waving on her shoulders and faintly perfumed. She gave him the special smile she reserved for him and his playful innuendoes and with a casual salute he drifted out.

But afterwards, unknown to Coult, she worked at the bookshelves with bright tears of anger and frustration in her eyes. Monday morning was looming up and soon she would have to take up the threads of her engineering life again. She needed strength to go on, and where was she going to find it with Todd always aiming for her weak spots? Always trying to make her feel like a woman when she had to think like a man.

CHAPTER EIGHT

WITH the full heat of the summer upon them the days at the mine were gruelling. The men worked stripped to the waist and Rennie bought herself a big straw hat from the compound store and some thin lawn shirts. Even so, at the end of the day she was soaked and limp with the heat. To sluice down under a tepid shower was to be re-born, if trudging in as though under a great weight was living.

And the evenings, when the earth exuded its strange exciting scents and the veld was awash with topaz light, only made things worse. To avoid being alone she drove over to Coult's house to help in the library, but more often than not they would end up sitting out on the veranda with a drink watching the sun, a torrid crimson ball, lowering behind the stark and ragged network of thorn trees.

Sometimes she dropped into the Crowthers'. The rollicking family atmosphere was balm to her wound-up nerves. She entered into twilight romps with Curt and Dory, though her body was often leaden with fatigue. She had the idea that if she wore herself out utterly each evening she would have little time to think.

She avoided Todd. Not that he was ever around, but she made a practice of locking up the engineer's office earlier than usual each night just to be sure. She didn't want to be reminded of her weakness, of the terrifying fact that her pulse could hammer sweetly in her veins at times, that her heart could draw tight with yearning.

Though, on occasion, it taxed her almost beyond endurance, she was glad of her work at the mine. Leith hadn't been too pleased about her taking time off, but he was too easy-going to let it worry him and as she had expected the jobs had piled up. It was the chief engineer who told her about the mine dance.

They were fixing new pulleys high up on an open stretch of belting at the field screening plant one morning when he called across to her with his uncouth grin, 'Heard about the big show on Saturday night? Our pals here,' he nodded to where the African labourers were working below, 'look pretty ordinary now, but wait until you see them in their feathers and warpaint.'

But is was Sylvia Crowther who explained all about the dance in detail. The large comfortable house had been undergoing a turn-out and the spare bedrooms were being aired and prettied up in readiness for the college daughters who were due home for their summer break, but Mrs Crowther loved a chat.

'There are over a dozen tribes at the mine,' she told Rennie, ironing daisy-patterned curtains. 'And each one has its own special effective type of dance. Each tribe demonstrates its accomplishments, and it's a kind of competition which provides entertainment for those who care to watch.'

Rennie smiled. 'You said that as though you weren't exactly keen yourself.'

Sylvia shrugged. 'I've seen dozens of mine dances in my time. They're set up by the authorities for several reasons. One is that the dances give the boys an opportunity to let off steam. I've seen them on the Rand, the real big ones. The girls—that's another matter. Patti's only eighteen. I wouldn't want her to go to one.'

'And yet you think I should witness the spectacle?' Rennie tilted an eyebrow humorously.

'You're a full grown woman, my dear,' Sylvia smiled. 'And besides it's an experience of a lifetime.'

Rennie was left to make what she could out of Mrs Crowther's cryptic remarks. Not that she was vitally interested in following the woman's advice. She had succeeded these past weeks, using rigid control, in shaping her life into a passable routine, her job taking precedence over everything. She wanted nothing to interfere with its precarious rhythm.

But on the following Saturday evening she wondered if she shouldn't after all take a stroll and see what was going on. She had watched the thorn-bush enclosure being constructed earlier in the day out there on the veld. Now huge fires licked at the stars, staining the sky with a salmon-pink glow. From the steps of her bungalow she could see in the distance the outline of passing figures bronzed by the firelight.

It was the drums that decided her. Throbbing, powerful, insistent, they drew her down the path and over the coarse grass, a kind of lure, a call that was too vaguely exciting to be ignored.

When she arrived on the scene the clearing, surrounded by groups of tamboutie trees, presented a fearsome yet riveting sight. The fires, shooting sparks up to the heavens, lit the intense, contorted expressions of the painted ebony figures, padding barefoot, swaying to and fro, to the thunderous, booming beat of the drums. She saw leopardskin anklets, blue plumes, ostrich feather headdresses, and not one mine worker did she recognise among the chanting tribe.

On the outer perimeter of the clearing were the forms and seats for the spectators. There was a large audience of Africans, mine employees and visitors and friends from outside. And practically all the hill settlement were there, the mine executives and their wives seated under the trailing tambouties.

One of the women, nervously eager to have the empty place between her and the outer darkness occupied, beckoned Rennie. She wandered over and sat down. Now that she was here, she might as well stay and watch. Indeed, she couldn't have dragged herself away.

The orange, satanic glow of the fires illuminating the glistening, contorting bodies of the dancers, their primitive vocal undersong, 'hooo—hooo ah—eeh', and the compelling, magnetic surge of the drum beat held her spellbound.

But that was only the start. After the Pondos, as she learned, doing their frenetic war dance, came the Amakwenkwes, who wore orange straps over their naked torsos, yellow shorts and white wool anklets. They rolled in the dirt, pranced with exaggerated movements, did turns like those of tumblers in a circus, and danced sitting down.

At the entry of the Amakwayas, wearing white feathers and carrying long tufted spears, she was sufficiently acclimatised to the pulsating scene to notice the differing facial characteristics of the performers, some with wide nostrils and thick lips, others with strong, aquiline noses and classic features, but all were glazed-eyed and mesmerised by the age-old rituals of the dance.

Tribe after tribe entered the arena, and like all shows when the music reaches a keener pitch and the rhythm accelerates there was a growing feeling of impending climax.

Rennie, flushed-faced and taut, went to quench her thirst at the refreshment table where there was fruit juice and other soft drinks. It was while she was returning to her seat that she caught sight for a few moments of the full contingent of settlement people, and standing with a group of executives across the clearing was Todd.

Whether he was in a position to have seen her from the moment she had arrived she couldn't have said, but he saw her now. And how could she help but see him? The smiling, indolent width of him, emblazoned as he was in her eyes against the grey nonentity of the crowd.

Of course she gave nothing away but cool recognition in her look, and to the profound, intensified throb of the drums she returned to her seat.

The Mandaws brought the show to a stealthy, frenzied conclusion. Naked except for loincloths, they were in full accord with the undercurrent of tense excitement which hung over the scene. Scarcely moving at first, they speeded up furtively, erotically, until the air seemed robbed of its life-giving qualities and the breath·lay imprisoned in the throat. Husky boys shuddered and veered and cavorted with wide grins urging on the clamour of the drums, and in turn the ever-quickening staccato beat drove them on to wilder contortions, increasing uninhibited rhythms, until the sweat poured down their faces, wearing away, as it were, the thin veil of civilised living and laying bare age-old and primitive desires.

Rennie wanted to turn away, to leave, but the music, pulsing, throbbing, its beat speeding up to a demoniacal climax, held her bewitched. It was the music of all Africa's primeval elements with its mystic overtones and nuances, and it was made poignant for her by memories of her own empty life, the aching absence of fire and feeling in her narrow workaday world.

At last the drums, hammering at fever pitch, crashed to an abrupt stop and the dancers slumped to the ground exhausted. Rennie slipped away through the trees. The fires had dropped low and their red ember glow was hardly sufficient to light the way, but she stumbled along quickly. Her heart was still pounding, the breath fluttering on her slightly parted lips, when the crackle of a footstep sounded on the rough grass ahead and a shape stepped out from the trees.

Todd was smiling faintly, that much she could see, but it was his eyes that seemed to reflect the dying flames of the fire. He was close to her before she could stir from the lethargy that gripped her and without a word he jerked her roughly into his arms.

In her present state the feel of his lips on hers inflamed her. She drained hungrily all that he gave. The bruising grip of his arms, the closeness of his hard male body fanned the greedy flame in her so that it became an all-consuming fire which coursed along her veins, making her senses sing with a feeling that was both pleasure and pain.

It was only when the holocaust lessened, when she awoke to the realisation that Todd's lips were still searching, wildly exploring hers, that she saw herself soft and pliable in his arms. She turned suddenly to steel then. Anger, both at him and her own weakness, made her push away from him violently.Tremblingly she tidied her hair and her eyes blazed as she looked at him and spat softly, 'I never thought it would be possible to hate anyone as much as I hate you!'

Todd's gaze was oddly lit. His grin taut and mocking, he drawled, 'Touched on a nerve, did I? Discovered that beneath the oiled-up dungarees and the peaked cap the old feminine instincts still survive?'

'For heaven's sake leave me alone!' she choked, thrusting a distracted hand through her hair.

'Gladly,' he rapped. Rennie could still feel the icy satire of his smile as she stumbled off into the darkness.

Shaking and ashamed, she made her way across the open ground back to the compound. She knew that he followed in her tracks, keeping a short distance behind her until she reached the safety of her bungalow. And once inside all the more reason to slam the door shut forcefully behind her.

The tears blinded her as she leaned against it. Todd was only out, for his own idle satisfaction, to prove that she was a woman. If only he had kissed her for some other reason!

CHAPTER NINE

IT was Coult Kramer who noticed Rennie's white, strained look. She had driven over shortly after finishing work one afternoon and eyeing her shrewdly where she had flopped in a chair opposite him on the veranda, a drink in her hand, a faraway look in her eye, he said without preamble, 'The job's geting you down, Rennie my girl. Why don't you come out with it and admit it! No one will hold it against you.'

'For heaven's sake, why does everyone *always have to keep on*!' As she jumped up and began to pace he watched her and stumped his foot. 'I'll have you know, young lady, that *I'm* the crotchety one round here. Now don't you go trying to steal my thunder.'

She turned, saw the look of roguish humour in his face and relaxed. 'I'm sorry, Coult,' she tried to smile. 'But this is something I have to work out for myself.'

'And you don't want an old-timer like me telling you your business, eh?' He looked at his watch. 'Too early for dinner yet. Get the backgammon board and let's have a go at the dice.'

She went inside to fetch the game and placing the board between them she dropped a kiss lightly on his cheek. 'Thank you Coult . . . for understanding.'

He snorted, 'Well, what are you waiting for, it's your throw,' but his eyes were soft and a little wistful.

These hours away from the mine were for Rennie a kind of release. Out on this lonely spot on the veld, chatting with Coult, losing herself in the engrossing task of cataloguing the books, she felt reasonably at peace. But not for long.

One afternoon when she drove into the grounds she noticed the familiar station wagon parked near the house. Voices were coming from the veranda as she approached and in the shade of the potted greenery she caught sight of the flame-haired, trouser-suited figure draped against a post. It was no surprise to find Lila at Vukasi. Her crazy stunt flying, centred over the hospital on her way in, was the talk of the mining community.

'Well, if it isn't our little apprentice! And not a smudge of oil to be seen.' She welcomed Rennie with her patronising smile. 'Coult's been showing me what a transformation you've made in the library. You ought to take it up, my pet. Machines are like horses, they can throw you when you least expect it.'

Not you too! Rennie sagged inwardly, but outwardly smiling she replied, 'Hello, Lila. Come to visit us rustics?'

'This is a thriving mine outfit. There's nothing rustic about the Vukasi diamond business.' Coult protested with his irascible humour. 'Come and sit down, girl.'

Todd, leaning near the doorway, drew up a chair for her. His expression lazily ironic, he asked, 'How was work today?'

'Smooth as always,' she lied, giving him a frigid look. She would never forgive him for that kiss.

Aaron, hovering discreetly in the background, brought

her a drink, and sitting back and sipping as though interested in its contents, Rennie listened to the chat which her arrival had temporarily disrupted.

'Maybe your diamonds are a pretty sight, Coult,' Lila took up where she had left off, 'but I tell you there's nothing to come up to a line-up of hundreds of gold bricks for taking the breath away.'

'Pshaw! Slabs of cold metal.' The mine owner waved away her argument and launched forth on his own. 'A diamond lives and breathes, and you know why? Because it's got the fires of the earth in its innards. Show a diamond the light of day and you switch on a divine radiance that, chances are, will outshine you and me and all else into eternity.'

'Ha! You're biased because you live among the things,' Lila pooh-poohed his clumsy attempts at poetry. 'A diamond man couldn't be expected to understand the miracle of pure gold.'

'Oh! And since when have you been in a position to compare the two? I bet you've never seen a crock full of diamonds just out of the acid.'

'There you are, you see!' Lila pounced. 'You talk of such things as divine radiance and then you bring in the messy business of acid.'

'And what about your thundering great furnaces? Tell me, is there anything aesthetic in the way you arrive at your "miracle"?'

The interplay was lively and conducted without animosity. Todd put in an opinion here and there, but he took no sides in the controversy. Rennie, sitting unobtrusively in the background, was struck by Lila's hairstyle. The russet tresses had been trimmed and fluffed out in a bunch of waves and curls on either side of her face. The central parting high-lighted the golden-winged eyebrows, but drew attention too to the heavy-lidded cynicism in her eyes and the drooping discontent of her full red lips. It was a trendy hairstyle, almost freakish on the ice-cool, precision-thinking Lila, and there was something in the bouncing blown up curls that suggested too a kind of exulting out and out defiance.

But more noticeable, to Rennie at least, was Lila's mood. Her voice was high-pitched and metallic as she fenced light-heartedly and cleverly with Coult. The cutting edge of her tongue was more than usually in evidence, although she practised laughing restraint when making her replies as though conscious of her own inner brittleness. There was nothing but that speed-ace confidence in her gestures, yet one got the feeling that she was living poised on the edge of her nerves.

It must be a condition in these parts, Rennie told herself wryly. Under cover of the conversation she was wondering how she could make her escape. Coult would think it odd if she made some excuse to leave, yet she had to get away. Todd's nearness was unbearable, the veiled taunt in his eyes when he looked at her altogether too much to endure. Then out of the blue a solution offered itself.

No one on the veranda had heard the approaching footsteps until Doctor Dunbar, medical bag in hand, appeared at the foot of the steps. The mine owner eyed him suspiciously and snorted, 'What the devil are you doing here, Peter? Not come in a working capacity, I hope.'

'Now, Coult,' the doctor soothed, 'you pay me to look after your health. I've been visiting a convalescent of mine in the end hostel block. As you were so near I thought I'd drop in and get it over with. Just a simple check-up. It won't take long.'

It was clear that he had had no idea that Lila was here. Though he smiled cheerfully as he spoke his face had paled noticeably at the sight of her and there was a taut white line around his mouth. 'Hello, Lila, Todd,' he greeted them perfunctorily, including Rennie in his smile and to the mine owner. 'Shall we go inside?'

'Not on your life!' Coult remained glued to his chair. 'You're not getting me in your clutches with that durned hocus-pocus. What you have to do you can do right here.'

'Just as you like,' the doctor, his usual urbanity asserting itself, agreed pleasantly. He opened his bag and placed various things on the table. While he was strapping up the mine owner's arm, Lila, who had been watching him with an openly derisive expression since his arrival, said with skittish humour, 'Would you take my blood pressure too, doctor! Flying high all the time I can't imagine what it must be like.'

His face was wearily severe. 'There's no cure for speed, Lila,' he replied bluntly. 'Your daredevil stunts over the hospital when you flew in yesterday were in extremely bad taste.'

'But, Peter dear, we're not all mummies lying in bed all day,' she smiled, innocently defensive.

'No, but you might have the decency to consider those who are subject to the misfortune.' He pumped up the blood pressure machine with methodical calm.

Something of a similar potent calm came through in Lila's manner as she replied lightly, 'Don't let it worry you, pet. I'm sure you've got enough humility for both of us.'

Rennie took an interest in her drink. She noticed that Todd stayed silent. Coult, who was watching the liquid in the machine near his arm jump up and down, exclaimed, 'The deuce! It's got more life in it than I have.'

The examination took only a few minutes. Putting away his things, Doctor Dunbar said smilingly, glancing over his report, 'Nothing to complain of. Keep off the hard drink, Coult, and we'll make an octogenarian of you yet.'

'The hard drink!' The mine owner showed offended disgust. 'Now when do I ever drink anything but fruit juice and coffee! Tell him, Rennie.' He met her twinkling gaze and with a sheepish chuckle owned up, 'Well, maybe the odd whisky and soda gets into my hand at times. And incidentally, Peter, what are you drinking now that you're through with your infernal instruments?'

'Can't stay, I'm afraid. A doctor is a busy man, you know.' He spoke evenly avoiding Lila's scornful smile. 'Perhaps another time.'

Rennie seized the opportunity and stood up. 'I've just remembered, Coult, I've got some letters to write.' Todd would see through her excuse, but what did it matter? 'As I'm driving back and the doctor doesn't appear to have any transport perhaps I could give him a lift?'

'A charming thought, Rennie, and one I mean to take you up on. The dust plays havoc with a fellow on foot.' Peter Dunbar snapped his bag shut and taking his leave of the others smilingly followed her down the steps.

Rennie, having waved goodbye to Coult, politely including his guests, could feel Lila's eyes burning a hole between her shoulder blades. She had noticed their look of veiled surprise at her rather impulsive suggestion, and afterwards their sudden calculating narrowness. Now that gaze, hard and brilliant, followed her as she left alongside Peter Dunbar.

The range truck was parked just inside the gates. The doctor took the seat beside her and soon they were out on the open grassland heading towards the compound. As they cruised along the avenue which led to the hospital Rennie said with a disbelieving smile, 'I didn't know you were an aspiring athlete as well as a doctor. It's quite a walk out here from the other side of the compound.'

'I thought the fresh air might do me good. I don't get enough of it, you know, working indoors.' That was his blithe explanation, but judging by the lines of utter weariness which crinkled his rather fine eyes she gathered that walking was for him yet another way of passing the time.

They drove in silence until the low roofs of the hospital came into view. 'Would you like me to drop you off at the entrance?' she asked, slowing imperceptibly.

'I'm free of duties until tomorow,' he indicated his house at the end of the block. 'It's home for me.'

So he wasn't as busy as he had made out. Rennie pulled up outside the gate where the walls were a tumble of blossom and sniffed ecstatically, 'Honeysuckle! I don't believe it!'

Doctor Dunbar climbed out and said with a tentative look at her, 'If those letters aren't too pressing you could come in for a while and have a look round. I'm insufferably proud of my garden.'

'I'd like to.' Knowing that she had nothing special to do either, Rennie agreed, smiling. She joined him on the pavement and he led the way inside.

The bungalow was of the usual works design, but there the similarity with the others in the compound ended. Its walls were a magnolia pink and a large semi-outdoor room had been added at the side. This overlooked spacious grounds which were a riot of colour and lush tropical growth.

Rennie was full of wonder and delight at what could be produced behind high sheltering fences, plus of course the endless patience required for this kind of horticulture. After the main garden Peter Dunbar led her to the back of the house to an area devoted to his fruit trees. Between the aisles she saw gnarled T-shaped branches on stubby trunks sprouting clusters of fresh green shoots and rows of spiky-looking shrubs with bandaged limbs.

'These are my patients out of working hours,' the doctor laughed. 'I'm having a go at paw-paw. The experts say the root of the tree married to an orange produces a rare and exotic type of fruit known as a paworange.'

Rennie looked intrigued. 'They would probably command quite a price on a rich man's table,' she commented as they turned back to the house.

'I wouldn't be surprised, but I'm only interested in the challenge.' He took her arm. 'If I ever arrive at the miracle

I'll let you be my guinea-pig and try the first one.'

'I'm game!' she laughed.

It occurred to her as they walked back along the path that her laughter was just as hollow and lifeless as Peter's. And the loneliness that came with the setting of the sun and the stirring of the night breezes showed in his eyes if not in her own.

At the steps leading to the garden room he said with his grave smile, 'Will you come in and have a sundowner with me? It's very pleasant sitting at this time of day.'

'All right,' Rennie consented lightly. What could she do? She sensed his keen desolation all the more because it was so much akin to her own mood.

They went up the short flight of steps into a tiled space where wickerwork armchairs and settee faced onto the open views of the garden. Drinks were brought by a servant boy and they sat, ostensibly content, breathing in the night-scented air and watching dusk weave its magic over the mine complex.

'No after-effects from your bump on the head, I hope?' Peter enquired conversationally after a considerable lapse of time.

'No, I've been fine,' Rennie replied. It wasn't her head that had suffered after her ride with Todd, she told herself bleakly.

After another lapse she asked, 'How are things at the hospital?'

'We've had a crop of minor cases,' the doctor smiled. 'The usual summer madness. The men go on terrific drinking bouts, then wonder when their bodies cave in.'

'What about the hill settlement?' Rennie asked. 'Do you get many calls from that quarter?'

'Only of a social kind,' Peter grimaced good-naturedly. 'These I try to avoid whenever possible.'

Rennie said nothing, but her smile communicated a

similar abhorrence for the sham existence of the hill so-
cialites.

'Unfortunately,' the doctor placed his glass down heavily
and gleamed, 'I'm roped in tomorrow night whether I like it
or not. It's the seventh anniversary of the birth of the
Kramer diamond mine and Frank Markson is having open
house.'

'Coult hasn't said anything about it,' Rennie remarked.

'He avoids these occasions like the plague, but unfortunately his henchmen are obliged to put in an appearance,'
Peter replied with a rueful grin.

Rennie looked sympathetic. After a while she finished her
drink and rose. 'I'd better be getting along. I've a hard day
ahead of me tomorrow.' She didn't say that an early night
was all she could think of to combat the slow disintegration
that was going on inside her.

The doctor got up. 'I'll come with you to the gate.'

The stars were noticeably bright in the amethyst glow of
the sky. Night birds swooped across the garden from the
open veld, speeding black shapes of chuttering sound. Peter
guided her along the path, a hand on her arm. At the gate
he didn't immediately let her go, and as she turned to him
enquiringly he said, a shyness mingling with his urbanity,
'Would you think it a frightful liberty if I asked you to ac-
company me to tomorrow night's anniversary celebrations?'

'Of course not,' Rennie said smilingly. 'I'd love to come.'
It wasn't exactly true. She had no desire to join in the
trendy activities of the hill settlement, but Peter obviously
needed someone and what harm would it do? 'What time
would you like me to present myself?' she asked lightly. 'I
can be here at your gate at any hour.'

'About nine o'clock, I think. Yes, that will be fine.' In the
semi-darkness he assisted her into the truck and as she
pulled away he said with a grateful look, 'Until tomorrow
night.'

Rennie drove back to her bungalow with a heavy heart. She had sworn she wouldn't let herself become emotionally involved while working at the Vukasi mine, and here she was involved up to her eyebrows. Peter was beginning to lean on her as a friend and what he felt for Lila she felt a thousand times more for Todd, if love could be measured. And there was no hope for either of them.

CHAPTER TEN

THE following evening when preparing for the night out Rennie got a sudden mood to dress up. Doctor Dunbar deserved something better than frayed jeans and old shirts, so rummaging in her trunk with tight-lipped determination she brought out an ankle-length dress in a creamy material with a lemon bouclé finish. It had slender shoulder straps and a silky saffron fringe just over the bosom designed to swish tantalisingly when the wearer walked. It took only a few minutes to freshen it up with a warm iron and later she was able to find lemon shoes and a jewelled evening bag to go with it. Heaven knew what had possessed her to pack such things in her trunk, but it showed she had never lost her true identity as a woman, she thought with grim amusement.

And so it was that, groomed and silken-haired and perfumed, albeit she had had to drive over in the range truck, she presented herself at the doctor's gate.

He was waiting for her, and as he guided her to his little blue car he said, 'You look very sweet, my dear. Far too charming for a dry old medical man like me.'

'You're neither dry nor old.' She eyed the debonair picture he made in his evening clothes and added with a twinkle, 'And I bet the majority of the wives in the hill settlement would agree with me.'

In outwardly gay mood they drove out of the mine compound and up the winding road among the luxurious white houses. But though the breeze coming in through the open windows was warm and laden with that indefinable earth scent that is Africa, Rennie's skin rippled with a peculiar apprehension. She didn't know why she should feel nervous about partnering Peter tonight, but something told her she hadn't acted wisely.

The Marksons' house was one of the grandest in the settlement. Its rooms, overlooking the steep drive and tumbling cactus flowering rockery, were ablaze with light, and sounds of the party in full swing came from the open windows. Inside the doorway a sign had been erected to commemorate the anniversary of the Kramer diamond mine, but its gaudy lettering, decorated by rhinestones to resemble diamonds, seemed to say that it was just another excuse for a celebration.

At these gatherings one just moved in with the crowd and drifted from room to room making conversation where one could and generally trying to blend in with the hilarity which to the outsider seemed to be mysteriously elusive. But Rennie had Peter for support. He was tall and good-looking in a grave, mature way and the females at the party couldn't get enough of his attention.

Rennie, for her part, created a sensation in a reverse sort of way. No one had ever seen Vukasi's girl engineer in anything but the rough outfits she used for her work, and the sight of her now, groomed and feminine, her hair in thick coils on her shoulders, brought looks of mild surprise and Rennie weathered the smiling, frigid reception outwardly immune. Like Peter, she was looking forward to the time when they could decently withdraw.

The whole of the hill settlement had turned up and the rooms were jammed with people. They made the rounds, entering into the lively chat here and there, accepting the drinks that were thrust upon them, always on the look-out for an available stretch of space in which to take a breather.

They spotted one at last. Near a draped window a shallow flight of steps curved round to a screened-off dais, a dining area perhaps where one could breakfast and contemplate the view. There were chairs there and—Rennie, leading the way, stopped dead at the sight of two people in the shadows, but it was too late to do anything about her blunder.

Todd and Lila appeared to have had the same notion about taking a breather from the party atmosphere. They were standing idly with their drinks screened by the vine-trailing fretwork. Rennie and the doctor had stepped into their view, so there was nothing for it but to make use of the spare space as originally intended.

Lila was over-bright in her welcome. Clad in a backless halter-necked dress in pale coffee, she looked a little thin and gaunt and her speech was slightly slurred. 'Well, if it isn't our good samaritan doctor, all dressed up to administer to the needy as always!'

As though to soften things Todd said, 'Hello, Peter, young Rennie. Enjoying the show?'

'Of course he's enjoying it, Todd! Have you ever known our dear doctor not to enjoy doing his precious duty?' There was a tell-tale tremor in the laughing, jeering remark. Rennie just didn't exist at the moment as far as Lila was concerned.

Peter, eyeing her swaying form, spoke evenly, 'A speed ace should never over-drink, Lila. You know that.'

'Oh! So I'm to be honoured with a diagnosis from our esteemed physician. You think I'm tight, doc? Well, well! Tell me more.'

Rennie turned to view the noisy party scene through the gaps in the fretwork greenery. There was something distasteful in listening to this kind of bickering. Todd drifted slightly away from the others too and came to stand beside her. He was wearing a green corduroy dinner jacket which made him look more the interior designer than the landscape architect. But that wasn't the only thing different about him tonight.

Rennie had sensed something in his mood from those first moments. Was it a damped-down, steely annoyance? His eyes certainly had a curious, hard light in them as he looked her over and commented with a twisted smile, 'So the chief engineer's got the brush-off tonight. Tell me, who was the guy who inspired the move, our good friend Pete?'

'I used to dress like this all the time before I came out here.' Rennie blithely ignored his all-encompassing appraisal. She hadn't forgotten that kiss, and she loathed his reference to her as 'young Rennie'. It seemed that if he couldn't take a knock at her engineering status he had to resort to treating her like a child.

'Why don't you do it now?' He eyed her quizzically. 'Afraid?'

'Of you?' She raised her chin scornfully, and in tones of withering amusement, 'Why do all men think they carry the death sting in their smile?'

'Maybe because the women like to think of us that way,' he drawled.

It was no note to continue on. The atmosphere was charged. There was something bordering on the inflammable in all their moods tonight, in hers and Todd's, and Lila's and Doctor Dunbar's.

Though all was bedlam and merriment out there in the party room there was no avoiding the tension this side of the screen. Lila's voice came to them, cutting and laced with laughing threat, '. . . you stick to patching the bodies, doc, and leave me to do the living. I promise you I'll do enough for both of us.'

Peter sounded jaded. 'Why must you flaunt with danger, Lila? Hurling yourself along the roads through the sky. Is there no other way you can get the maximum fun out of life?'

'Fun! What do you know about fun?' came the taunting reply. 'You with your dedicated ideals ...'

Rennie turned. It was time to go. She waited at the edge of the steps, but Lila was a long way from being through. 'What kind of a kick do you get out of life, dear doc, living in your world of the sick with one foot in the mortuary?'

'A doctor has his job to do,' Peter said steadily.

'I know all about the Hippocratic oath.' Lila wore a ghastly smile, her eyes were abnormally brilliant. 'Well, I took one too, and do you know what ... you know ...' Her brain dulled by drink, she seemed to lose the thread of what she had been going to say, and as her voice broke Todd moved swiftly to her side. His tones were gentle as he put an arm round her. 'Come on, Lila. I'll take you home.'

Rennie didn't know why she should feel it so strongly, but as Todd looked at her face before he led Lila away she somehow sensed that he blamed her for the scene. There was a door in the shadows not far from the steps and discreetly he guided Lila through and shut the door quietly behind him.

Peter was haggard. Rennie felt limp. But as they stepped out to mingle with the others in the room they were spotted by Sylvia Crowther. 'Rennie, my love!' She came over, just a little tipsy. 'I hardly recognised you. What a sweet dress! You look delicious.'

'Thank you, Sylvia.' Rennie forced a smile and tried to appear chatty. 'Is Martin here?'

'Somewhere, dear,' Mrs Crowther replied cryptically. 'He has a habit of hiding himself away with a newspaper on these occasions.'

'Oh well! Give him my love,' said Rennie, hinting at their departure. But by this time Sylvia had collared Peter. 'And Doctor Dunbar!' she pumped his hand. 'It's ages since I've seen you at one of our gatherings. How's life at the hospital these days?'

'Can't grumble.' He tried to sound courteous, then lead-Rennie off, 'You'll excuse us if we dash, Mrs Crowther? Pressing business, you know.'

'Oh, a patient. I see.' Sylvia looked vaguely understanding and gave them a wave. 'Well, cheerio you two.'

Out on the drive Peter sagged with relief. Rennie was aware of her quivering nerves. They made the journey back to the mine compound in silence. Down by the hospital the doctor parked outside the gate of his house. Alarmed at the putty green of his features, Rennie got out of the car first and went round to open his side. She took his arm on the pavement and they went along the garden path together.

It was late and the house, though lit, appeared to be deserted. They went in the front entrance into a living room with plain furniture and folkweave covers. The doctor dropped down into an armchair and lowered his head into his hands and Rennie, white-faced too, felt that there was nothing more she could do. But as she turned to go he caught her hand in one of his and raising his head said with an apologetic, twisted smile, 'You're entitled to an explanation, my dear. It couldn't have been very easy for you, standing by and listening to Lila's not very charming invectives.'

Nothing had been easy for her tonight, her emotions raw Rennie recalled Todd's acrimonious, controlled mood which had clashed abrasively with her own. She longed for the privacy of her bachelor hut so that she could give in to the weight of her unhappiness, but the look Peter gave her was pleading, so consenting she took a nearby chair.

'You probably don't know this,' he said, running a hand through his hair, 'but Lila and I were engaged once.'

'No, I didn't know that,' Rennie murmured, somewhat taken aback by this rather startling statement.

He nodded, slackening his tie jerkily. 'I worked in the big city hospital in Johannesburg in those days. Lila's father was brought in with a minor heart aliment and we got to know each other during his convalescence.'

'What happened?' Rennie asked softly.

'We almost married,' he shrugged with a bitter look. 'But Lila had always taken it for granted that I would join her father in the gold business. When I told her that I would never give up the medical profession, she couldn't take it. She's always had a phobia about illness and a dread of being an invalid.' He looked racked. 'There were the usual rows and finally the break-up.'

The picture grew clearer and Rennie said gently, 'It doesn't explain what you're doing here at the Vukasi mine hospital.'

'Doesn't it?' His smile was crooked with implication. 'Lila's never been crossed in her life. We may have agreed to part, but she's never given up the idea of trying to convince me that a doctor's life is a morbid existence. In the end I had to leave the Johannesburg hospital . . . to get away . . . I found, a position in a small hospital in a Transvaal farming community, but Lila's father is powerful and influential and through him she soon found me. So . . .' his sigh was eloquent, 'I took this job at the mine hospital and later discovered that Lila's father had brought Rosedale less than a mile away. Since then I've refused to do any more moving on . . .'

'What you mean,' Rennie said, with gentle understanding, 'is that you don't want to keep running away from Lila.'

He didn't answer this, but she knew by his tortured look that he was still very deeply in love with Lila. Then lifting his head he said with a worn smile, 'It wouldn't do any good. She likes to let me know she's around and that she's getting the most out of her life.'

'Her flying, you mean, and racing powerful cars?' Rennie nodded, knowing what hell he must go through on Lila's behalf.

'And all the other wild sports she can find to indulge in to prove that a doctor's life is staid and unimaginable,' he said with a cracked laugh.

Poor Peter! What a mess. 'Does Todd know?' Rennie asked.

'Todd knows, but he minds his own business. He's Lila's friend and he's my friend and he won't take sides.'

Rennie's heart missed a beat. 'But I thought Todd and Lila were something more than friends?' she said in a low voice.

'Perhaps they are ... perhaps that's what she wants ...' Peter ran his hands distractedly through his hair. 'I just don't know any more.'

He had a pallor that worried Rennie. She rose and poured him a stiff drink from the bottles on a nearby cabinet. When she took it to him he said with grimacing humour, 'The patient attending to the doctor!' But he drank it down and after a while his colour returned. He looked up to where Rennie stood beside him and said with a grateful grin, 'It's been good talking to you, my dear. Thank you for staying.'

'I'm glad I could help a little,' she replied softly. Her lingering concern must have been evident, for he reassured her with a brusque smile, 'Don't worry about me. I'm used to these bouts. Tomorrow I'll be back at my job and it will be just so much more water under the bridge.'

'Well, if you're sure ...' she moved shyly to the door and he rose. 'Of course. What a selfish brute I am—you look flaked out yourself. Goodnight, Rennie,' he squeezed her shoulders briefly, 'and thanks again.'

Rennie found her way out to her range truck and drove through the night-shrouded compound leadenly piecing together what she had heard. Lila and Peter were like poison to each other, but they couldn't shake each other off. It was later, however, her head on the pillow and sleep evading her that the question came to gnaw at her torn emotions.

Was Todd standing by Lila in the hope that she would one day get Peter out of her system and turn to him?

Things were not going very well at the mine. The hot, searing high-veld winds played havoc with a man's nerves and tempers at the quarry face were quick to flare. The only sure way to get through the punishing, sweating dust-filled day was to think of the fun to be had at the end of it. Rennie, nursing her own private miseries, thought that the men were a little too eager to down tools in favour of the beer gardens in the residential compounds. But Leith was the boss of their division and she kept her opinions to herself.

She often wondered afterwards if the disastrous outcome of this lax attitude could have been prevented if she had stood her ground and spoken her piece. But maybe, she admitted to herself, with her heart a dead weight inside her, she was in a lax frame of mind herself. And she had become so used to muddling through on Leith's behalf she had stopped having nightmares about the possibilities of a major calamity. If only she had kept this dreaded possibility to the forefront of her mind!

They were handling dynamite that fateful afternoon. But there was nothing in the air to suggest that it was anything other than a normal working day. The men were looking forward to knocking off shortly and everyone was keen to get the job done and be through. Even Rennie's mind tended to jump ahead to the time when she would be free to sluice away the dust under a cool shower. It was only when she saw the way the work was going that she began to get the first stirring of unease.

The dynamite crew were still packing the tubes in the kimberlite rock. The light was fading and to her mind they were cutting things rather fine. She was used to Leith's somewhat hazy timing of these jobs. The bombshell came when she heard him call out breezily, 'Okay, boys, you can knock off now. Time to call it a day.'

She waited until they were alone at the site office and then spoke in incredulous undertones. 'You're not just going to leave everything until morning!'

'There's not much else we can do now, kid. Too dark to go through with it tonight,' Leith, rapidly peeling off his overalls, told her good-naturedly.

'But the detonator heads are in position,' she said with a faint gasp.

'I know that,' he shrugged easily. 'But so what? The area's cordoned off, and nothing's going to happen until we connect to the plunger box. And who's going to go nosing around a pile of rock littered with dynamite notices?'

'But suposing there's a loose pebble, or a small ground animal disturbs one of the detonator heads?' Rennie asked nervously.

'Well, so what! They'd just be doing the job for us.' He laughed his raucous laugh while running a comb through his hair. Then anchoring her with his gaze he said patiently, 'Look, you know as well as I do that it's better to blast early in the morning when the earth-moving machines can move straight in. Now relax. I've told you everything's okay. You worry too much, kid.' Passably spruce after his quick change, he gave her a reassuring slap on the back, then climbed into his truck and shot away noisily, heading for the residential compound.

Rennie watched the men pile into the mine buses and when the area was deserted she pondered on what Leith had said. It was true the area was cordoned off. And no one was allowed in the quarrying section after dark anyway, so perhaps she did worry too much. With a sigh she took one last look at the red flags flapping languidly in the breeze in the distance and then turned towards her truck.

By the time she had reached the residential compound she had made peace with herself concerning Leith's somewhat cliff-hanging way of handling things. After all, he was the chief engineer, and he had years of experience behind him. At the corner sink, in the vehicles shed, she washed away the worst of the day's grime, then trudged into the engineer's office to make out her report.

As they were later finishing tonight it wasn't long before all the work chits had been handed in and her own duties completed and she was free to go. What made her linger she couldn't have said. Some odd, unfathomable instinct perhaps. She often recalled that evening and wondered, her blood turning cold, what would have happened if she had locked up the office there and then and gone to her bungalow.

As it was she stayed to clear up. The desk was cluttered with all kinds of mess that didn't belong there and it would take her but a few minutes, she decided, to neaten things a little. She had got rid of the old bits of wire, mislaid tools and discarded machine tickets and was putting away a couple of outdated ledgers when her eyes fell on the geologist's report tucked away in one of the lower drawers of the desk. She scanned it idly, wondering what to do with the ledgers. Suddenly something she saw there held her rooted.

The ground seemed to sway beneath her. Her nerves tingling she had to sit down to take in the horrifying details which seemed to scream at her now from the pages of the report. *Blasting precautions for Area B*. Area B? Wasn't that *where the dynamite was just waiting to be ignited*? Her hands trembling, the blood rushing to her head, dazzling her vision, she could hardly take in the technical implications laid out before her ... a fissure of monolithic pivotal rock formations extending for a distance of six miles in an east-west direction ... danger of collapsing terrain ...

A fissure of pivotal rock. She knew what that meant. One tiny explosion would be enough to start off an underground reaction which would flatten the six-mile monolithic chain like a line of stacked cards. And in an east-west direction. Her heart stopped dead. *That was towards the residential compound and the hill settlement*. Oh, heavens! She jumped up from the chair. One small ignition would be enough to destroy the whole mine complex. Houses would collapse and —— She fought to overcome the panic that threatened to turn her bones to water. She had to find Leith, and quick!

Outside she flung herself into the range truck and swerved lurchingly out on to the dusty road. It was almost dark now. If only she had discovered the geologist's report earlier! So much precious time had been lost. If so much as a beetle crossed in the path of one of those detonators ... Her temples damp, the tears in her throat, she schooled herself into concentrating on action. It was the only way she could keep from going completely to pieces.

At the open-air beer garden she pulled up sharply and hurried in at the main entrance. The lights spilled out under the trees, over the drink-slopped tables and garden greenery, and she was hailed by the wine-happy mine employees. 'Hey, Rennie! Come and join us. What are you having to drink?'

'No time now, boys.' She tried to sound normal. 'I'm looking for the chief engineer. Is he here?'

'The chief!' The exclamations were accompanied by whoops of throaty laughter and knowing looks. 'He was here. Try round the back. Our Casanova pal likes a little privacy.'

Rennie took the path they indicated. She spotted Leith standing in a pool of light under a young acacia, but her hopes sank when she saw his great bulk swaying like a reed in the wind. 'Leith!' She made an attempt to shock him out of his inebriated condition. 'Something very serious has happened. We have to go to the quarry site at once.'

'Worsh a matter, youngster?' He eyed her with bleary good humour in between tossing darts unsteadily into the dartboard hung on the tree. 'You wanna work at thish crazy hour ...?'

'I don't *want* to ...' She shot a tortured smile at the shy figure sitting nearby. She knew Magnolia, an attractive girl from the riverside village. '. . . It's just that we have no choice. It's to do with the geologist's report. We have to go and de-cap the dynamite immediately.'

Patiently the chief engineer rested his great hands on her shoulders and breathed his beery breath on her cheek. 'Look, honey! I told you, everythingsh all right. Now go away like a good kid and gimme some peace, huh!'

Rennie gave up. It was a waste of precious time. And Leith was in no fit state to handle the tricky detonator heads anyway. Leaving him squinting bemusedly at the bull's eye along the end of his wavering dart, she went back out to the truck. There was nothing for it; she would have to tackle the risky job of removing those detonator head herself.

It was only when she was bumping along the mine road towards the quarry site that the horrifying realisation of what she was about to take on hit her. Going hot and cold by turn, she knew that one false move with a detonator stick of dynamite and . . .

To steady her shaking hands she tried to think of something else. She ought to have been on her way over to the house on the veld. Coult was expecting her. They had completed the cataloguing of all the books and tonight was to have been a kind of celebration to mark the neat and orderly layout of the library. Well, it would have to wait until later. If there *was* a later. Grimly she swung the truck towards the quarry boundary. But first she had to get past the security trailer.

It *would* have to be Ted Mills on guard duty tonight! Heavily built and respectful, late of the London police force, he had the ponderous, inmovable attitude of a granite boulder. 'I'm sorry, miss, you know the rules. No one goes into the quarry area after dark.'

'But, Ted, this is an emergency!' Rennie bit back her exasperation. 'There's something very important I have to do.'

'Then it will have to wait till morning.' The rock didn't budge. 'The ground's littered with diamonds in there. It would be more than my job's worth, miss, to let anyone past this check-point without proper authorisation.'

'If I wait for that you might find the diamonds the least of your worries,' Rennie retorted with frustrated, macabre humour, and recklessly she slammed her foot on the accelerator.

'Here! You come back here, miss!' His ponderous dignity affronted, the ex-policeman waved his arms at her.

'I will, Ted. Just as soon as I've finished,' she called soothingly.

The encounter had dulled her mind to what lay ahead, but once out where the star-filled sky and a paltry thin sliver of moon shed their scanty light on the scene the enormity of the job she had set herself turned her legs weak.

The cordoned-off area, with its red flags just visible in the gloom, lay in ghostly stillness. She could see the ledge of rock marked out for blasting on the outer lip of the quarry. She would have to manoeuvre herself along the lower ledge and take each cylindrical hole in turn. Five of them there were, and each packed tight with lethal explosive. Though she knew now how crazy Leith had been to leave such a situation to simmer over until morning, her emotions were mixed. Supposing he had decided to get the blasting over with before they knocked off work!

Pacing at the edge of the quarry, her nerves jumping, she suddenly woke up to the fact that she had rushed over completely empty-handed. What a fool! Dazed by shock at the geologist's report, she hadn't thought to pick up her tool box. And a torch—at least she would need a torch. Wringing her hands, she had a thought. The site office might have one.

Quickly she drove over the uneven ground to the white-painted hut in the distance. Inside there was all kinds of junk on the shelves, but groping her hands came upon nothing remotely resembling a torch. She checked again. Her brow was damp and she knew inwardly that she was only trying to put off the evil moment.

Gritting her teeth, she drove back to the quarry. She would have to do it by the headlights of the range truck. And she needed nothing but her hands, cool and steady and unfumbling. She looked at them in despair. If only they would stop shaking! If only she could steel herself into some kind of lasting composure.

The lights were trained on the cylindrical cavities and she stared at the impassive detonator heads glinting innocently there. But each time she plucked up the courage to make an attempt her legs gave way under her. Her mind might have been tuned to what she had to do, but her body let her down. It was then, after countless abortive starts towards the detonator heads, that she knew her failings. The sobs escaping from her throat, running her hands wildly through her hair, she knew she couldn't do it. It needed a steady hand for so delicate an operation, and she was a hopeless, dithering wreck.

She was pacing, pleading to the heavens for help, when she saw the headlights of a car, twin beams reaching out into the darkness as it nosed its way over the rough ground towards the quarry site. Rennie's heart leapt. Had her words got through to Leith after all? Had he sobered himself up sufficiently to come and take charge of this nightmare situation?

She waited palpitatingly as the car drew nearer. She was blinded by the headlights. She heard it jerk to a stop and the car door slammed as someone got out. The figure was hazy in the contrasting blackness ... but didn't she recognise that crisp footstep?

She watched the dark shape move into the lights of the truck and groaned, 'Not you!'

Todd took one look at her overwrought state and rapped,

'What's going on? What in heaven's name are you doing out here all on your own?'

'What are *you* doing here?' she counter-questioned, sagging literally at the sight of him.

'Ted Mills rang up Coult to report a forced entry at the quarry. I'd been invited over ... something about a celebration dinner ... I told him I'd come out and investigate.'

Rennie digested the staccato explanation. The phone on Coult's desk in the living room. She knew how he hated it, but he answered it on the infrequent occasions when someone wanted to get in touch with him at the mine. And despite her agitation she knew an acute sense of disappointment at the thought of missing dinner when Todd had been going to join them.

His gaze searching now he was quick to detect the desperation in her and eyeing the red flags he asked tightly, 'What's wrong? What fool job are you trying to attempt in a danger zone?'

She pushed the tumbling hair out of her face and said swaying wearily, 'It's a long story ... I came across some information in the office concerning area B.' She waved an arm at the flags. 'The geologist's report mentions pivotal rock formations and a danger of collapsing terrain.'

'I've seen that report,' Todd nodded. 'They advised a counter-blast at the opposite end of the fissure using the "bridge-quarry" effect.'

'I know, but this advice was ... overlooked,' she confessed feebly. 'Normal blasting has been set up for morning and the dynamite's live, just waiting to be ignited.'

'Ye gods!' Todd exclaimed softly, and in the same breath, 'Switch off the truck lights.' Rennie was slow to react and swiftly moving ahead of her he said when they were in complete darkness, 'If anyone gets a whisper of this we could have a full-scale panic on our hands.'

'I know.' Rennie chewed her lip. 'A flash cave-in, in a direct line with the mine complex.'

Todd paced in the gloom. 'Where the hell is Leith?' he snapped.

'It's no good calling Leith,' she said heavily. 'He's past it. For tonight anyway.'

'Soaked, I suppose,' Todd said grimly. 'And the rest of the dynamite crew with him, no doubt.'

'I came to unscrew the detonator heads.' Rennie glanced wildly in the direction of the flags and shook her head in despair. 'But I found I couldn't do it.' She looked towards the twinkling lights of the mine complex and suggested numbly, 'Should we evacuate the houses, do you think?'

'No time for that.' Todd listened to the wind rattling the dry gravel in the ditches and began to roll up his shirt sleeves. 'You'll have to show me where the bore holes are.'

'You!' Rennie looked at him in a daze. 'But . . . I'm the engineer.'

'So you keep telling us.' She saw his warped smile in the gloom and the look he spared for her trembling frame. 'I've got a torch in the car,' he flexed his fingers ready for action. 'Reckon you can hold it still enough for me to see what I'm doing?'

'I . . . I think so.' She stumbled after him as he went to get the things he would need. Then for the twentieth time that night she ducked under the rope of the cordoned-off area, only now Todd was with her and her fears were not only for herself but for him. Feeling faint but fighting the nausea, she led the way down to the rocky ledge where the bore holes were ominously visible in the beam of the torch.

Todd crouched before the first one, carefully weighing up the situation as she held the heavy torch with both hands. Crouched by the side of him she had never felt closer to him than she did now—or more confident. Compared to her own limp state everything about him seemed to suggest latent strength, his powerful shoulders, the width of his throat, the strong flexibility of his wrists. He inhaled deeply, gave her a long meaningful look, then muttered with a grin, 'Well, here goes!'

Rennie's heart stopped its wild pounding when he placed his fingers delicately on the detonator cap and began to turn. It flew up into her throat and stayed there suffocating her with its noisy throb in time to each turn of the screw. She felt she couldn't hold her breath another second when—oh, joy!—the detonator head parted company with the explosive and lay safely in Todd's hand.

'You did it!' she gasped, meeting his gaze in sheer disbelief.

'Never underestimate a landscape gardener,' he said in his laconic style.

They moved on to the next hole. Rennie's hands were damp around the torch, but she was heartened now. All it needed was an iron nerve and a rock-like composure, and Todd possessed both. The minutes ticked by and relief hovered on the brink of their moods as he moved along the line of holes. 'Three down, two to go.'

Rennie collected the fourth cap. Soon now she could start thinking about sweet life again. She expected no more problems. Then Todd said in tones that twanged at her nerves again, 'The last dynamite stick ... I can't reach the cap.'

'You can't what!' The torch began to dance in her hands. She stared at the cylindrical cavity and saw the detonator head snuggling back in the interior.

Todd looked at her. She knew he was thinking that her hands were smaller than his. She shrank back. 'It's no good asking me to do it,' she choked. 'You know I couldn't.'

He bit his lip pensively, then nodded to the oddments of tools he had brought from the car. 'Pass me the small file.'

'You're not going to ...?' Horror in her gaze, she did as he asked mechanically.

'We have no choice,' he said practically. 'I'll have to file away the lip of rock ... enough to give me a finger-hold.'

Rennie closed her eyes at the rasping sound. Would the nightmare never end! She counted the seconds as Todd worked, and each one seemed to last a year. Supposing he nicked the live dynamite with the tip of the file! But he wouldn't, would he? she prayed. Nothing could happen now, could it?

'You're moving the light,' Todd said crisply. She opened her eyes and saw that he was about to attempt the de-capping. *One screw . . . two screws . . . three . . . four.* 'That's got it!' he breathed as the cap fell into his hands.

'Oh!' Rennie was speechless. She hid her face in her arm to hide her emotion and dropping the torch stumbled up the rocky path of the quarry and out under the starlit sky. Anywhere to be alone. She heard Todd methodically gather up the bits and pieces and return them to his car. Then he came to stand beside her on the open veld. 'Relax,' he said gently. 'It's all over.'

She swung on him. 'I wasn't much use, was I?' Her voice shook with emotion.

He shrugged. 'Don't take it too much to heart. You're an engineer, not an explosive expert.'

'I'm an engineer and I hate it, hate it, hate it! . . .' As she buckled under the intolerable strain of the evening all the bottled-up unhappiness of the past months suddenly broke loose. Her eyes brilliant with tears she moved like one de-mented.

'Well, well,' Todd said softly.

Tossing her hair out of her eyes, Rennie turned and told him with theatrical matter of factness. 'Fate allowed my parents one child—me.' And with a catch in her voice, 'Do you know what it's like being the daughter of a famous man, knowing that he wanted a son? The Rennerton name in engineering must be handed down to future generations and all members of the family must shine under the illustri-ous——'

'Rennerton!' Todd snapped his fingers. 'Sir John Rennerton. He was given a knighthood a few years back for his work on the Sydney harbour bridge.'

'He's just big Jack Rennerton to his friends,' Rennie said with a mirthless smile.

Todd whistled softly under his breath. 'So the old boy pinned all his hopes on you?'

'You think that kind of thing only happens in fiction,' she shot him a bitter gleam. 'Well, you're wrong. I can tell you that when you're an only child and your father wants nothing but the best from you, you move heaven and earth to please him.'

'Now I get the Rennie bit,' Todd said after a pause. 'Why the secrecy?'

'A son wouldn't want to trade on his father's name, a daughter even less so.' She gave him her splintered smile, then jerkily paced again. 'I wanted to be a good engineer ... but I just haven't got what it takes.'

'Stop whipping yourself,' Todd said harshly. 'You've got a lot more than most.'

She slowed to a halt then. A new emotion shone dimly through her tears. Coming from him this was praise indeed!

She felt spent and sank down on the crackling turf to rest against a slight rise. Todd came to join her. Relaxing beside her, he said lightly, 'If Rennerton's your surname, you must have another one.'

'I have,' she replied, calmer now. 'I was christened Spring.' And with the shadow of her drawn smile, 'That was my mother's idea.'

'Spring Rennerton,' he said it slowly, musingly. 'It's a pretty name.'

'But unusable in my case,' she made a face. 'Have you ever heard of an engineer being called Spring!'

'Yes ... I see what you mean,' Todd grinned. Then with a slight tightening of his expression he re-capped on what she had told him, 'So your father decided you were going to follow in his footsteps and you went through with it ... the studying, the exams, the whole works, against your will?'

She plucked a blade of grass. 'It sounds crazy, doesn't it? But when you love someone you'll do anything.'

The grass brittle in her fingers, she became aware for the first time of her surroundings, the hot, earthy smell of the veld, the breeze rustling through the stubble and the black shapes of trees, and the all-encompassing darkness. She lay back and breathed a long, imperceptible sigh. She was at peace now. Todd knew, and as he stretched out beside her and clasped his hands under his head, she felt light enough to float up and away.

A long time later, viewing the breathless display of stars above them she said dreamily, 'Coult's gems scattered over the sky. What do the adverts tell us? A diamond is forever ... Love is a diamond ...'

Close to her Todd wore a contradictory smile. 'Love is the brightest star,' he pointed it out for her. 'It outshines all other emotions.'

Rennie's heart skipped a beat. She had been talking earlier about her love for her father, about deep family ties. Now she was a little confused. 'What kind of love?' she asked faintly.

'The kind between a man and a woman,' Todd said vibrantly.

The silence of the veld washed over them. Somewhere a night bird warbled at the waning moon. They lay for some moments longer, then Todd took her hand and pulled her up. 'Come on, I'll drive you back. We'll leave the range truck here tonight. I'll have it delivered to your place in the morning.'

Her hand in his, she went with him lightheadedly to his car. As they drove back towards the mine complex with its twinkling lights she knew a kind of delayed and blissful relief. The houses were safe now. The blasting would be carried out, taking the necessary precautions, in the morning, and there would be no more danger of collapsing terrain.

The lights became powerful street lights overhead and all too soon she saw that they were driving along her own deserted stretch of road. Todd pulled up outside her bungalow and hazily she felt his hand on her arm. 'Get some sleep,' he said, gently propelling her towards the path. 'I'll tell Coult we had a small problem with an earth-moving machine on the soft edge of the quarry.'

She heard him drive away and as she moved indoors she gazed up bemusedly at the velvet sky. *Love is the brightest star. It outshines all other emotions.* What had Todd meant by those words?

CHAPTER ELEVEN

WHAT transpired between Todd and the chief engineer Rennie never learned. But Leith was a changed man. He supervised the blasting the following day with meticulous care and an occasional white-faced, sheepish look in her direction. And he never left her to do a job on her own again.

The celebration dinner with Coult was put back slightly because something happened to make the dinner serve two purposes.

When Rennie drove over to the house on the veld a couple of days later the mine owner eyed her with a secretive twinkle. 'Still holding out on us, on what part of the world you come from eh?' he chortled. And with a mysterious air, 'Well, I reckon I can fill in those missing details on your works record any time I like.'

As Rennie blinked, lost for words, he pulled a letter out of his pocket and waved it under her nose. 'This came this morning. It was sent to me from the offices of Sir John

Rennerton.' At Rennie's gasp he smirked, 'Oh, you recognise the name, do you!' And making a great show of
putting on his spectacles he flicked through the contents.
'It seems he's doing a lightning educational tour of South
Africa, and he wants to know if he can drop in and see his
daughter in between lecture dates.'

'Father coming here!' Rennie received the news with
mixed feelings.

'Naturally he's eager to see how his prize chick is making
out,' said Coult, his smile a little set. 'He and his wife will be
flying in for an overnight stop tomorrow afternoon.'

'So soon!' Rennie looked agitated. 'But where am I going
to put them? My bungalow is much too——'

'They can stay here' Coult waved away her worries.
'There's plenty of spare rooms.'

'Here!' Now it was Rennie's turn to twinkle back at him.
Her hands on her waist, she confronted him with amused
severity. 'I can remember the time when you wouldn't see a
soul. Now you're so gregarious I can't keep up with you.'

'It's you who teaches me these bad habits,' he chuckled,
turning away.

The following afternoon they were waiting on the air strip
when the small plane landed. Martin and Sylvia Crowther
were there and Todd had strolled over from his house
minutes before. The door of the plane was opened and out
stepped the big, thick-set figure that Rennie knew so well,
and behind him a woman of the same slender build as herself.

Coult handled the greetings. His white hair lifting a little
in the wind, his stooping frame frail looking at the side of
the stalwart figure in khaki drill, he put out a hand. 'I'm
Coult Kramer, the mine owner.' And indicating the
others, 'This is my mine manager, Martin Crowther ... and
his wife. Todd Dillman here is a personal friend of mine.'

Todd shook his powerful hand. 'It's a pleasure to meet
you, sir.'

Rennie had come straight from the mine and dusty in working gear she stood dutifully waiting until her turn came round. 'Hello, Daddy.' His remorseless gaze raked her as he put out a hand to counter any display of affection and instead of hugging him she stood and shook his hand like the lowly works employee that she was.

Her mother stepped forward then. 'Hello, dear. You're looking thinner.' They embraced affectionately and Lady Rennerton got somewhat carried away with an excited account of their travels. 'What a time we had making the jump from the Cape Town college to the one in Pretoria! They laid on a car for us and we were doing over a hundred on the Kimberley-Johannesburg road, and Jack said——'

'No time for female gossip now, Jessie,' the big man shut her up. 'We're only here for a few hours, and if these gentlemen will kindly lead the way I'd very much like to take a look round the mine.'

They made for the cars. Sylvia, chattering happily with Lady Rennerton, guided her towards Martin's vehicle. Rennie sat beside her father in Coult's Landrover, with the mine owner at the front and Todd at the wheel. It was open house for the V.I.P.s at the mine. The guards were spruced up at the security check points and stood to attention as the cars went by.

Alighting amidst the dust and clatter of the quarry workings, Rennie felt her father's stringent gaze on her. 'Now let's see what young Rennerton's learned about the mining business.' By this she gathered that she was expected to lead the tour.

She did her best, pointing out the different quarrying methods, and the machines that were used for each operation, but occasionally she stumbled over the name of an important machine part or a mechnical term and this would bring an impatient rebuke from her father. 'Come, come, gal! This is an open-cast mine. You wouldn't use cone-shaped excavation unless you were going six hundred feet down.'

With the other men he was hearty and talkative and insisted that everyone call him Jack. But Coult treated him with a certain amount of reserve, and Todd's gaze was occasionally frosty. Lady Rennerton, very much under the thumb of her husband, was compelled to stumble along on the dusty tour, though she wasn't remotely interested in mining—diamonds or otherwise. But Sylvia was virtually intrigued by the other woman's mode of living, so they gossiped animatedly together and took little notice of their surroundings.

After the quarry they did a tour of the field screening and recovery plants. Rennie was a little shaky here because she spent most of her working hours out of doors. Inevitably she fell down on the names and functions of some of the mechnical devices designed for recovering diamonds. Her father would settle for nothing less than perfection. 'It seems to me you've learned precious little during your months out here,' he remarked austerely at one point.

Todd was close by. With a smile to soften his terse tones he put in, 'On the contrary, sir, your daughter has a very extensive knowledge of the mining business. I doubt whether you at her age could have remembered the precise nut and screw in every component.' Jack Rennerton viewed him with his ruthless stare and moved on.

At the end of the tour Rennie had to get back to work. The afternoon was only half over and there was no such thing as taking time off to be with her parents. Her father wouldn't have heard of it. Martin went thankfully back to his office and took Sylvia off with him. As Rennie moved off towards the quarry Todd said in aside tones with an encouraging grin, before driving Coult and his guests back to the house, 'See you tonight at dinner.'

That grin put the seal on Rennie's mood for the evening. After work she showered leisurely and later luxuriated in the feel of silky underwear next to her skin. In a cloud of apple blossom perfume she slipped into a dress which had been brightened to a dazzling crispness by a hot iron. It was simple, yet girlishly feminine, having a nipped-in waist and a flouncing knee-length skirt, and it was patterned delicately with multi-coloured, pastel-tinted flowers. Her hair she brushed into gleaming waves, and allowed it to fall naturally on either side of the lace-edged horseshoe neckline.

It was true her hands trembled a little at the wheel of the range truck on the way over to the house on the veld. But she had only to think of Todd and all her misgivings about the way she looked dissolved. It was dark when she arrived. Lights spilled out from the veranda. She could hear the men's voices inside as she took the steps in her slender-heeled-sandals.

She made her entrance casual and slightly detached as though she always tripped about frothily dressed in the middle hours of the evening. The group were sitting around in the living room. Coult didn't bat an eyelid except to say, 'Ah! Here's our fifth for dinner.'

Todd, who had changed into a pale tropical lounge suit, rose and the hint of mischief in his gaze connecting with hers he drawled 'Well, it looks as though the wait was worthwhile.'

'You look positively enchanting, darling!' The words were out before she could stop them and Lady Rennerton shot a penitent glance at her husband and then to cover her embarrassment patted the seat beside her. 'Come and sit here by me, dear.'

'Can't stop up all night.' Rennie's father rose. 'Due for an early start in the morning. If the meal's ready we might as well go in.'

Coult led the way through into a room which had obviously been set aside for the rare occasions when he entertained. The others followed and Lady Rennerton, on Todd's arm, talked animatedly about the things she had seen during their stay in South Africa. But any such light conversation that crept in during dinner was brutally pushed aside to make way for technical chat. Rennie's father saw to that. He was here on a working tour not that he ever travelled any other way—and he and his pet theme, engineering, dominated the talk which accompanied the various courses at the table.

Coult, who for some time had been at pains to remain civil, obligingly aired his knowledge of the mining business. Todd proved, as he had on several occasions, that he knew quite a bit about machinery. Rennie of course was dragged into it all, for wasn't this just her father's way of testing her to see how much she knew. That she failed miserably in his estimation on many occasions throughout the meal, she was well aware. And she sensed too—hadn't it been more than apparent since she had stepped in at the front door?—his withering disapproval of her feminine attire.

His mounting dissatisfaction came to a head when, in telling her mother a little about the mine dances, she lost the thread of his conversation and flunked when he chose that moment to a fire leading question at her. Still in his khaki drill, he fastened his iron-hard gaze on her and remarked, 'Slipping, aren't you, gal!'—He always called her gal, deprived as he was from using the familiar term 'son'— 'That kind of poser was child's play to you in England.' And making no secret now of his distaste for her appearance. 'I'm not sure I like the way you're handling yourself out here. Titivating yourself up like a fancy wedding cake and filling your head with useless information on local customs won't get you those important letters after your name.'

Todd lowered his knife and fork with studied calm. He said lazily, 'You've got a very attractive daughter, Jack. Why not let nature have its own way?'

'Nature doesn't come into my scheme of things, Todd,' came the hardy reply. 'The gal here's poised for a brilliant engineering career. It's up to me to steer her in the right direction.'

'*Your* direction,' Todd said with a smile. Coult concentrated on paring his apple. Lady Rennerton dabbed at imaginary coffee stains on the tablecloth. Todd continued in the same steely, smiling tones, 'Have you ever asked your daughter what *she* would like to do with her life?'

'Never had to,' thick-skinned and jocular, Jack Rennerton replied. 'She's her father's child. Followed in my footsteps since she was small.'

'Could be that this was just love and loyalty, Jack. But you wouldn't see that. You've worked so long with machines you've become one yourself.'

The atmosphere at the table might have become electric had big Jack Rennerton been a man of feeling. But, oblivious to the veiled criticism in Todd's tones or any real point to the conversation, he puffed on his cigar and told him benignly, 'You'll get married and have children yourself one day, Todd, then you'll know what I'm talking about.'

'Maybe, but I don't see myself as a tyrannical father pushing daughters into jobs that don't suit them,' came the suave reply.

The cigar smoke between them, for the first time those marble cold eyes rested thoughtfully on Todd. Rennie said hastily, 'I think I'd like another cup of coffee. What about you, Mother?'

'Now there's an idea!' Coult exclaimed on a waft of relief. 'Why don't we all have another cup of coffee?'

Aaron brought in a fresh pot and the conversation became general for a while until Rennie's father looked at his watch and told her, 'Well, gal, we won't keep you from the sleep you need for your job. Your mother and I will be retiring shortly, so don't feel you have to hang on, on our account.'

Rennie, recognising this as her dismissal, rose and said her goodnights. Her parents came out on the veranda with her to bid her farewell as they would be off at dawn in the morning. 'It's been wonderful seeing you, darling.' Her mother hugged her close, a note of regret in her voice that so much had been left unsaid between them.

Ignoring his outstretched hand, Rennie embraced her father. 'Goodbye, Daddy. Enjoy the rest of your South African tour.'

'I will. Lecturing in technical institutes is my strong point,' he said heartily, and with hardly a backward glance as he turned indoors, 'And don't forget, the best present you can give me is the news that you've got that next engineering diploma.'

Waving to them, she ran lightly down the steps and over to her range truck. Her cheeks were flushed as she drove back to her bungalow in something of a dream. It was a state that continued long after she had undressed and got into bed. Her eyes shining, she lay and stared into the darkness, her happiness too great to contain. Todd had taken her side. Todd had gone out of his way to stand up to her father on her account.

The plane flew out the next morning and all traces of the V.I.P.s was obliterated as the vapour from the machine disappeared into the blue.

Coult regarded the interlude as one best forgotten and this he promptly did. He was developing a penchant for going places and whenever Rennie had a spare moment she would invariably find herself at the wheel of the Landrover. They went to Tombaza and poked around the market there, unearthing dubious treasures from the piles of African bric-à-brac on the stalls, and explored the native villages alongside the river Zamba.

One afternoon the mine owner borrowed one of Todd's boys, a tall young native in bush jacket and shorts, wearing a knife in a sheath fashioned out of the foot of an antelope, and they drove over to the Aasvogel Arena. They cruised along the tracks in this primitive, forgotten world, and stopped in hideaway places to wait for views of the wild game coming to drink at the rock pools. While they were watching a waterbuck step delicately down the path in the wake of a herd of wildebeest Coult said, 'I'm thinking of organising a safari day out here. The shooting season's well under way and Frank Markson and some of the other men are itching to get at their rifles.'

Moshuto in the front seat kept a wary eye on the waving feathery grasses near the car and Rennie eyed the many tracks which disappeared into the shimmering, tangled undergrowth. She could understand this kind of sport going down well with the excitement-starved hill executives. They followed the skittish antics of a troop of young zebras and laughed at the strutting ludicrous walk of a pair of ostriches, and Coult said, 'A whole day here would be enough to put on a bit of a show for you.'

'For me?' Rennie exclaimed. And with affection, 'Coult, you're always doing things for me.'

'Why shouldn't I if I get a kick out of it?' He frowned furiously at a passing family of water hogs. Then ducking and shooting her his misty-eyed twinkle, he muttered, 'You know somethin'?' He fumbled with the pocket on the car door. 'If I'd had a daughter, I would have wanted her to be just like you.'

'Are you sure you wouldn't have preferred a son?' Rennie said, a hint of bitterness behind her smile.

'Nope. A daughter would have suited me just fine.'

Her arm in his, Rennie murmured softly, 'Coult, you say the nicest things!'

In between chasing over the countryside there was her work at the mine. The day after the Aasvogel run, however, this was brought to a stop at midday. Aaron, of all people, drove out to the quarry site and told her that Coult

wanted her to come over for lunch. She alighted from the
Landrover at the house on the veld and seeing Coult waiting for her on the veranda she scolded lightly, 'I'm a working girl, remember. I haven't time to indulge in all this high
living.'

'No buts, Rennie.' Though he spoke jokingly there was
something like a slow, kindling excitement in the mine
owner's manner. Casually he took her arm. 'This is kind of
a special day for me. This afternoon I'm going to show you
what you mine in the raw and how they look on the
sorters' tables—diamonds!'

After lunch they drove over to the mining area and
parked outside the sorting house. Though Rennie had done
one or two maintenance jobs around the place she had
never been into the sacred domain where the actual diamonds were graded, for no one was allowed in here except
the specialised workers. Now Coult led her along clinical
white corridors and eventually, after much locking and un-
locking of steel doors by security staff, they stepped into a
large room, a kind of oversized, barred cage, where African
boys sat near the windows poring over the job of sorting
rough diamonds.

Down the centre of the room long padded-topped tables
held neat piles of graded diamonds in rows, some no bigger
than a penny, other piles as big as an upturned washbowl.
Leading her along, Coult pointed to one of these washbowl
heaps of glittering gems and told her, 'A few weeks' production from the Kramer diamond mine. Talking in my
currency, there's maybe a hundred million dollars there.'

Rennie gasped softly, lost for words. He showed her the
four main categories on the sorting tables. ' "Stones", that's
what we call diamonds of a fairly regular shape, "cleavages",
those are irregular-shaped broken crystals. Then there's
"maccles", triangular-shaped twinned diamonds, and "flats"
which are thin flat crystals.'

Were all these fantastic jewels what they grubbed each

day out of the ground, hardly noticing them, or caring, as they were dumped amidst tons of rock and gravel into the hoppers at the separation plant! Rennie saw a miner's work now, with a new eye. After the tables Coult showed her the diamonds being weighed on electronic scales and the machines they were trying out which could sort the stones through colour and shape. It was an interesting tour, but Rennie wasn't clear as to why the mine owner should suddenly take it into his head to show her his incredible wealth.

As they drove back to the house he didn't leave the subject there. 'The Kramer diamond mine is extraordinary—almost unique, you might say,' he told Rennie with that look of pride. 'In the first place the diamonds are predominantly gem stones—none of your industrials here. In the second, they lie almost on the surface of the earth just waiting to be scratched out like a chicken pecks at grain. Most South African mines are underground and are expensive to work. Thirdly, the deposit here in Vukasi is fabulously rich. In other mines you can expect to get six to eight carats per hundred cubic yards of earth. We average two hundred and fifty to three hundred and fifty carats a day.'

When they got back to the house Rennie's mind turned to work. But Coult was in a lingering mood, that inspired look and secretive gleam more than ever apparent. He ordered drinks and they sat on the veranda listening to the distant hum of the mine machinery.

'Reckon you know something about the diamond business now, Rennie my girl.' He spoke more into his drink than to her.

'I should say so!' she laughed. 'Served up on the tables like that they certainly are a fabulous sight.'

'I'm glad you think so—well, who wouldn't?' he chuckled into his glass and then at her, 'because ... well ...' He put his drink on the table and got up and stopping his pacing shot a misty glance at her. 'I've got nobody but a no-good cousin in Johannesburg ... and ... doggone it!' He sat down again decisively and took her hand in his. 'Rennie my girl, I've decided to make you my heir ... heir to the Kramer diamond mine fortune!'

'Coult!' Rennie gasped, bowled over by the news. She sat there slightly open-mouthed, trying to take in the full implication of his words, but her mind wouldn't work.

Delighted with himself now that his secret was out, he chortled, 'It'll take a day or two, I know, to get used to the idea, but you can take it from me, it's no dream. If anything happens to me the mine's yours.'

Her eyes brimming with affection, Rennie choked on a laugh. 'What can I say except that I don't deserve it!'

He held her hand in his, and said quietly, but with a certain intensity, 'You taught me a lesson in living. One that I'm never gonna forget.' Then, embarrassed by his own sentimentality, he brusquely made the change back to his cockahoop mood. 'I've already asked the office to contact my lawyers in the city. We'll be getting the will and the papers drawn up in the next few days. In the meantime,' he eyed her with his roguish twinkle, 'you can carry on being a working girl. It'll give you something to take your mind off the shock.'

'Heavens, don't I need it!' She rose with a dazed smile, and cornering him before he could step away she put her arms round his neck and rested her cheek on his. 'Thank you, Coult, for everything,' she said softly. 'And if I'd have been able to choose my father he would have been like you.' She left him then, knowing that he would be fighting to keep the damp from his eyes.

Back at the quarry site she drifted about in a whirl for a while, then pulling herself together she gave all her attention to the job in hand. And curiously enough she soon forgot all about Coult's news. But if she had pushed all thoughts of being a diamond mine heiress to the back o her mind, it was evident that the mine settlement was mildly astir at the idea.

The news must have leaked out from the offices, for after that day, wherever she went, whether she was on her way to work or shopping in the compound supermarket, she would find herself being eyed with smiling interest and lighthearted envy. She was well liked around the mine complex and everyone seemed to be pleased for her.

Rennie soon got used to the stares. She knew the news would be a seven-days' wonder. As it happened something occurred, a dreadful tragedy which took her mind clean away from her own affairs.

They had been expecting trouble for some time among the miners. But as often happens fate made this a mere smokescreen to disguise what really lay in store.

Johann Wenhold and Otto Lange had been at each other's throats for a long time. Things came to a head when Susy Wenhold, who had once been courted by Otto, made a car trip with some of the other wives down to Pretoria, for a lark. It happened that Otto had been away from the mine at the same time, supposedly visiting a sick relative in the city. Johann accused him of playing around with his wife, and Otto hotly denied it.

Both parties had been spoiling for a fight all day. They were guilty too of drinking on the job. The fact that Johann worked in the ore-washing plant was no deterrent. He was not short on excuses for making trips to the quarry site. To cool them down both were kept busy at back breaking tasks, but towards the end of the afternoon no one could keep them apart any longer.

Luckily by this time both were so unsteady on their feet that there was little danger of harm being done. Unfortunately Otto, in bracing himself swayingly for contact with the glowering Johann, caught his foot on the rubber ridge of a track-type bulldozer and was catapulted over the edge of the quarry. It was only a four-foot drop, but he had fallen awkwardly and lay gasping with pain, unable to move. Rennie was the only one nearby with transport. She was quickly dispatched to the hospital to fetch Doctor Dunbar.

When they returned Otto was in a sitting position, pale but more or less himself. 'A twisted back by the look of it.' Doctor Dunbar examined him with stringent humour. 'That'll teach you to get fish-happy on the edge of a drop!' He helped him to his feet and walked him back and forth gently to make sure that no real damage had been done. Then closing his bag he said, 'Get a light job for a couple of days, Otto. And if you have any trouble come to the hospital and I'll give you some liniment.'

The miners dispersed. Work was finished for the day. There was no sign of Johann. He had been spirited away by his mates, no doubt, to be jokingly lectured on the futility of losing one's temper.

Rennie said to the doctor, 'I'll drive you back.'

Beside her in the little range truck he murmured with a teasing smile, 'How does it feel to know you could be driving a diamond-studded Cadillac one day?'

'I hardly ever give it a thought,' she replied truthfully. And with a laugh at her dusty appearance, 'I'm still Rennie the engineer!'

She dropped him outside the hospital, where he lingered, holding the handle of the truck door. 'I'll be handing over to Doctor Mulandzi in a few minutes,' he told her. 'Will you come over to the house and have a meal with me?'

'What, like this!' She looked down humorously at her grubby dungarees, at the same time wondering what kind of a reply she should make. She was itching to get over to Coult's. Todd would be dropping in any evening and every part of her was aching to see him again. But she didn't want to be offhand with Peter. And perhaps she needn't stay too long after the meal. She glanced at her watch. 'I've got to go to the engineer's office and clear up the day's work,' she explained. 'I can wash up there and be back here in about half an hour.'

'Wonderful!' Peter breathed, squeezing her hand with that grateful look.

She rattled away in the truck and watched him walk with bowed head into the hospital grounds.

He was waiting for her at the gate of his house when she returned, fresh in tee-shirt and jeans, later. There was enough of the evening left to enjoy a stroll round the garden, and the doctor showed her the latest developments in his fruit tree section. Rennie enthused over everything. She felt she had to. Her heart contracted every time she looked at Peter. His face, those grave, gentle features that could at times be lit with a carefree boyish warmth, were lined and drawn and she knew what he was going through. Lila had driven up from the city in her super-powered sports machine and spent her time tearing back and forth along the roads between the nearby towns. Often in the dead of night, when all was still in the mine complex, the powerful engine of her car could be heard shattering the silence of the veld.

'Shall we go in and see if dinner's ready?' His smile quietly masked all he felt as he took Rennie's hand in the gathering shadows now and led her up the steps to the garden room. At the table set for two, the heavy scent of oleander wafting in from the night shrouded flower beds, they ate salad and a couple of South African dishes, *bobotie* and *melktert*, laid on for Rennie's benefit. The doctor talked about the isolated cases of malaria and local fevers that they sometimes got in the hospital and Rennie chatted about her work around the mine.

Afterwards they retired to the armchairs to linger with an after-dinner drink. While Peter was pouring Rennie took a peep at her watch. It was just after nine, reasonably early still. Peter came to hand her her glass. He was looking more relaxed, and she was happy that she had been able to do that for him. As they sat back, facing each other, she said, keeping up the lighthearted mood, 'By the way, whatever happened to the native boy you had in the hospital, the one with the evil spirit on him? I never did find out.'

'Oh, young Zebb Gugushe!' the doctor laughed. 'You're not going to believe this, but the quarrel for which he was calmly forfeiting his life concerned nothing more than——'

His cheerful explanation was drowned in the harsh shrieking of brakes as a car jerked to a stop outside the gate. They both got up to look through the window aperture. 'Now what?' the doctor asked heavily, noticing the medical conveyance in the shadows. Hearing the running footsteps on the path Rennie wondered too, with a slightly quickening heart beat, what could be the matter. Was something wrong at the hospital? Had Johann and Otto come to blows after all?

It was Darrell who took the steps two at a time up to them where they stood in the garden room. His face was as white as a sheet and gulping in breaths, it was several seconds before he could speak. And what he said didn't seem to make much sense. '... Joshua and another orderly were driving back from town. Khoto has relatives in the village on the left bank of the river ... they were turning off on the road just past the bridge ...'

In an effort to help Rennie cut in firmly, 'What is it, Darrell? Has there been an accident?'

The young man slumped and nodding shot a look at the doctor. 'It's Lila Harwood. They found her car overturned near an old baobab tree. By the look of it they think she hit it.'

Rennie was afraid to look at Peter. She did so momentarily and saw, as he clasped a chair for support, grey-faced and shrunken, that he had become the mere shell of a man. She asked the question for him. 'Is she ... dead?'

'No ...' Darrell, young and sensitive, was hardly the type to deliver bad news. He struggled on, '...but she's pretty terribly injured. Joshua sent Khoto back for help and has stayed to do what he can.' He flicked another embarrassed glance at the swaying man. 'They thought at the hospital that Doctor Dunbar should be told.'

Rennie nodded and pulled herself together. 'You'll need your bag, Peter.' Gently she laid an encouraging hand on his arm. 'And some drugs perhaps from the hospital.' Her fingers gripped him, willing him out of his shock, and he came to and nodded briskly. 'You're right. There's no time to lose.'

Rapidly she helped him on with his jacket and asked, 'Would I be of any use?'

'No.' As he turned to go he squeezed her hand and mingling with the haggardness and dread in his face the light of something inexpressibly tender shone through. 'You've done enough.'

Rennie watched him go with a lump in her throat and she knew that that look on his face would remain with her for ever.

When the car had left she went through the house to tell the servant boy that the doctor had been called away, but to clear away the dinner dishes as usual. Then she drove over to Coult's. The mine owner showed no great surprise when he heard about Lila. 'Always been a highly strung girl,' he said, shaking his head sadly. 'Dicing with danger in those scientific speed machines her fool father buys for her. It's a wonder to me she's stayed in one piece as long as she has.'

They hovered near the phone and got a little news through. Todd had been told and had waited at the junction of the mine road for Peter and followed behind him in his car to the scene of the accident.

There was no further communication. It grew late and, weary after the shattering events of the evening, Rennie said goodnight to Coult and drove back to her bungalow.

News of the accident and what had happened afterwards

trickled through in bits round the mine complex the next day. Once on the spot Doctor Dunbar had decided there and then to get Lila straight to the hospital in Johannesburg. He and Joshua had taken turns at the wheel of the car and arrived in the early hours of the morning. Lila had been rushed to the intensive care unit. She was holding her own and it was thought that she would survive.

There were daily bulletins after that giving accounts of Lila's slow fight back to life. But as all this was happening far away and didn't touch on the lives of those at the mine settlement the tragedy soon began to fade from people's minds. The summer sun carved out the mountains in molten blue against the pearly heat of the sky. The African dusk cast its soft purple veil over the bushveld and life around the mine complex returned to normal.

Rennie was eager to see Todd. So much had happened since their last meeting when her father had made his flying visit to the mine. But it couldn't be long now that everything was on an even keel again. She hung on in the engineer's office each night, sometimes until it was almost dark, in the hope that she would hear that familiar footstep. When he didn't appear she drove over to Coult's and drifted about the living room holding her breath for the sound of his car.

Mooning there one evening, she said as casually as she could, for she knew that Todd was planning to bring the mine owner some book information he needed concerning his valuable first editions, 'I thought we might have had a caller tonight.'

'Todd, you mean?' Coult looked up from his newspaper. 'He was here earlier this afternoon.'

Rennie bit back her disappointment. He had dropped in while she was at work. Well, she wasn't too downhearted. Tomorrow was Saturday and she was free all day. Todd knew that.

Fresh in rose pink slacks and white shirt, she hurried over to Coult's after lunch the next day. The heat was not so intense and with sky winds pushing balls of white cloud across the blue expanse of sky and the veld a sweep of metallic gold under the spreading acacias, it was a gorgeous afternoon. With singing pulses she gazed out expectantly from the veranda, but by four o'clock her eyes had grown tired of watching the road from the open gateway. After that she resorted to drifting back and forth, fingering the plants in half-hearted interest and whirling round at the slightest sound out there in the grounds.

Coult had eyed her fidgeting from time to time. He said at last, putting his book down and shooting her a wily gleam, 'If Todd's too busy to pay us a visit, why don't we go and call on him?'

'Oh, could we?' Rennie blushed and tried to tone down her eagerness.

'I don't see why not.' The mine owner kept a straight face as he rose. 'Rosedale happens to be close by, and we've got the transport.'

Rennie had never felt so happy as she did in those moments when they were cruising along the road outside the mine gates. The banks of the jade-green river were fringed with bamboo and feathery rushes, and with the luxuriant flowering trees, to her the route had never looked more beautiful. They turned in at the Rosedale gates and drew up on the circular drive fronting the house. Todd's car was there and Rennie felt the sweet excitement coursing through her veins, though it was all she could do to contain her impatience she waited until Coult had unhurriedly extricated himself from the Landrover. By that time there was no need to go in search of Todd. His head and shoulders appeared along a path leading up from the lower gardens. He was instructing a group of African workers who were gingerly transporting a consignment of new trees.

Her heart in her eyes, Rennie went with Coult down the

path. Todd, in rough slacks and shirt, looked up as they approached. 'Well, well! So the one-time recluse has taken to making social calls. Hello, young Rennie. Go easy with that sapling, boys—it took seven years to grow to its present height.'

'How's the work going, Todd?' Coult glanced around him with interest. 'This place sure has changed since the last time I was here.'

'We're putting in a line of ornamentals on the western outlook. Come on down and take a look around.'

Beyond the lily pool, beside a newly erected summer house, Todd showed them the latest developments. Rennie said, catching a glimpse of sun-dappled waters beyond the rose hedge, 'I never knew there was a swimming pool in the grounds.'

'Didn't I show it to you the last time you were here?' Todd crouched to check on the roots of a sapling just laid down, then rose to his feet. 'Yes, there's a swimming pool, and a wild garden, and, believe it or not, a children's garden.'

As they strolled he pointed out various touches, explained the operations in hand and those yet to be attempted. After a while Coult said, 'By the way, Todd, did I tell you that the safari I'm organising for some of the mine executives and Rennie here to show her a little of the raw African life is more or less all fixed up? You'll join us, of course?'

'Sorry, Coult,' Todd checked on the label of a tree coming in on the shoulders of two boys, 'this stuff's got to go into the ground as soon as possible. It's been a long time on the road.'

The mine owner squinted at him from where he stood. 'You can't make it, huh?'

'I'd like to, Coult, but pressure of work, you know,' Todd shrugged, and stuck his pencil behind his ear.

'Sure, I understand.' The mine owner turned back along

the path and added with a grin, 'We'll tell you all about it when we get back.'

Todd came with them as far as the foot of the rise back up to the terrace. 'If you want refreshments just call in at the house,' he pointed to the open door. 'It's very pleasant sitting with a drink on the stoep.'

Coult said drily, puffing a little, 'When I get to the top, it's me for the Landrover and home. How about you, Rennie?'

She nodded. 'I think I'd rather wait for a drink.'

'Well, so long, you two. It was nice showing you around.' Todd gave them a salute and turned back to his work.

Out on the road Coult went out of his way to say chattily, 'Quite a show piece, that Rosedale. It's hard to believe that those gardens were once raw bushveld.'

At the wheel Rennie said nothing. But perhaps he saw the glisten of tears in her eyes, because he asked abruptly, 'What's the matter, girl? It's not the end of the world because Todd's not coming with us on the safari.'

'Of course it isn't.' She blinked away the wet brilliance and gazed fixedly at the road. 'It doesn't matter to me whether Todd comes on the safari or not.' All she wanted to do was get back to the mine complex; to forget the whole sorry escapade. Oh, it was true there was nothing to label it as a disastrous visit. Todd had been his old charming self, laconic as always and even a little teasing as he had pointed out items of interest to her. But she had sensed an aloofness in him, an impassive withdrawal, and slowly, as she hung on to his glance, his smile, a cold and cruel ache had crept in to disperse the bubbling joy in her. Now, driving back along the river road, it was hard to keep the tears from blinding her. She should have known. It was Lila he loved. Her car accident had shaken him and now she was with Peter in Johannesburg. Clearly Todd was throwing himself into his work at Rosedale to forget.

Instead of the delicate impala lilies at the roadside Rennie saw herself lying under the stars at the quarry site with Todd, sitting across from him at the dinner table with her father, and the memories only served to increase her devastating misery. She had been fooling herself that Todd cared for her in some small way, when all the time his mind had been on Lila.

CHAPTER TWELVE

RENNIE tried to hide her feelings for Coult's sake. After their visit to Rosedale she put herself out to appear carefree and serene. She went into the kitchen and taught Aaron how to make her favourite English dishes for the mine owner's approval and filled the rooms of the house with flowers, much to the disgust of Romaano, who had a hard time growing them in the arid grounds.

She thought up an improvement for their filing system in the library and made herself generally available for chat or playing backgammon. But she had a feeling that Coult wasn't fooled. She knew he watched her as she nervily straightened up the things on his desk or re-positioned a potted plant. On one occasion he lowered his city newspaper, giving up the idea of concentration, and told her, 'That lamp standard has stood on that square of mat for nigh on seven years. I reckon it's got used to the spot by now.'

'Sorry.' Rennie affected a light air. 'I just thought I'd move it out of the corner a little.'

'Well, I think it's fine where it is.' His stubbornness bringing things to a head, he eyed her piercingly and a little perplexed asked as she turned away, 'Aren't you happy . . .? You've got the mine.'

'Of course I'm happy, Coult.' She went to drop a kiss on

his cheek. 'You've given me everything.' How could she tell him? Without Todd the diamonds meant nothing to her. And if she had Todd's love she wouldn't need them. Her eyes were bright with unshed tears as she went to potter about in another part of the room, knowing that Coult followed her with his piercing gaze.

At the mine there was no need to struggle quite so hard to put on a smile. Work was work and everyone went about it according to their mood. If Rennie had lost that vital spark no one noticed. One night when she got back to the bungalow something odd happened.

She had spent the evening washing out a few smalls and generally tidying up and was planning on having an early night. After a light supper she was leaving the kitchen to go to the bedroom and there it was, a folded note lying on the floor by the front door as though someone had pushed it underneath from outside.

Her first reaction was to open the door and look out. But there was nothing but the dark night outside and the rolling starlit grassland across from the doorway. How strange! Whoever had been must have made the trip on foot, for she would surely have heard the car. She closed the door again and locked it securely, then slowly unfolded the note.

The message was printed in untidy block letters. Rennie read it, cocked an ear to see if she could hear any retreating footsteps, then read it again.

You're not wanted around the Kramer diamond mine. If you know what's good for you pack your things and get out.

What a peculiar note! She folded it with a set smile. If this was someone's idea of a joke she didn't think it was very funny. Tucking the note into the pocket of her jeans, she tried the front door once more, then went off to undress for bed. The following morning she rose, breakfasted and drove over to the quarry site as usual.

The African sun, though tempered by the high-veld

winds, used none of the workers kindly and it was always a relief to get to the end of another day. Rennie, numbed with unhappiness, hardly noticed the trying conditions. The heat of the day, the cool of the evening, it made no difference to her heartache.

One late afternoon when she was driving back from the mine she heard a shout from one of the bachelor bungalows. Among the few that were inhabited at this end of the road she knew that Darrell lived in one, and it was he who waved to her from his doorway. When she got out and went up the path she saw that he was holding something in his hand.

'I've been looking for you,' he said with a shy grin. 'I wanted to give you this before I leave.'

'Leave?' Rennie echoed the words, her face crumpling. 'Darrell, you're not——'

'No, I'm not pulling out of South Africa,' he said with a laugh. 'I'm going to the hospital in Johannesburg to train as a male nurse. Doctor Dunbar arranged it before he left.'

'So you're really going in for the medical side,' Rennie smiled her relief. 'I'm glad, Darrell. I think you'll do well.' She looked at the framed picture he had given her. It was a charcoal sketch, the head of an African youth executed simply but with impact, for the lines had captured the arrogant beauty in the ebony black face. 'It's wonderful.' She held it to her. 'I shall treasure it always.'

A little pink with embarrassment, he nodded indoors. 'I'm just packing up. Come on in.'

Rennie wandered into rooms, small and simply furnished like her own. 'How are you travelling?' she asked.

'Ted Mills is flying down with a consignment of diamonds for the vault in the city bank. I'm not supposed to know that,' Darrell slung some things into a holdall and sloped a smile. 'I'm just getting a lift.'

Rennie examined some more sketches propped up beside

the table. 'You know, these are really good. You should do something about that talent of yours.'

Darrell shrugged off her enthusiasm goodnaturedly. 'There are thousands of artists. My stuff would probably sink without trace among the least successful of them.'

Rennie didn't agree, but she didn't argue. They had a drink together and she helped him to round up lost socks and things, then in the doorway she shook his hand, 'Well, goodbye, Darrell. I do wish you luck in your new life.'

'Cheerio.' He squeezed her hand lingeringly and added shyly, 'And thanks, Rennie, for your encouragement.'

'Me?' She put on a bright smile though her throat ached. 'Todd Dillman was the prime mover, I believe, in moulding your new career.'

He nodded. 'I'll be writing to Mr Dillman from Johannesburg.'

They went down the path together and before she climbed into the truck Rennie said, 'Perhaps you'll change your mind about training to become a male nurse when you get to the hospital. You might decide to enrol as a medical student.'

He closed the door on her, shaking his head with his self-effacing smile. 'I'd never make a doctor.'

Rennie stifled a sigh. That was Darrell—always underplaying himself. One day he would meet a girl who would make him feel more sure of himself and then he would start to go places. She waved to him as she drove away and he waved back until she turned the bend out of sight.

Darrell's going left a miserable void in Rennie's life. Though she hadn't got to know him very well, and they had met only a few times in the mine complex, he was, like her, recently out from England and there had been a kind of bond between them. She missed him to the point of black despondency.

Perhaps because of this mood she felt drawn towards the

doctor's house. It was all locked up now. Peter had been reinstated at the Johannesburg hospital and held an important position there. He wouldn't be coming back. Wandering around the garden, already shabbily overgrown, she was touched by the melancholy of things left behind as their owner moved on. Would the new doctor give a thought to Peter's fruit trees, now sadly in need of attention? She doubted it.

Heavily, in the dusk, she made her way back to the range truck. She was just going to get in when something caught her eye on the door. Something white. It was a note and it had been slotted in the ledge of the turned down window. Rennie felt a chill as she unfolded it. She recognised the untidy block letters.

That last note was no joke. Accidents happen around the mine. You'd better leave. NOW.

Rennie folded the note, shivering a little. She looked around. The road was deserted, yet someone must have stolen along within these last few minutes and tucked the note in the truck window. But who? The lonely thoroughfare was no place to figure out such a question and quickly she drove back to her bungalow.

Once inside she pondered over the mystery. Who would want to get rid of her? As far as she knew she had no enemies in the mine complex. What about the hill settlement? Had the news that Coult had left her the diamond mine in his will upset one of the executives' wives? She smiled at the thought. It was highly unlikely. Their husbands earned fantastic salaries and money was the one thing that none of them were short of. No, she was going round in circles, and as there was no sensible explanation the best thing she could do was to forget it. Once the practical joker discovered that there was no reaction to his pranks the thing would fizzle out. Just the same, she double-checked when she locked the outside door for the night.

She stayed away from Coult's house during that working

week. It was too much of a strain trying to keep up a smiling front, especially as he followed her with his pensive gaze. She heard from Aaron in the compound supermarket that the mine owner had made a couple of visits to Rosedale to see Todd. This was natural enough, she told herself dully. The two men were close friends and no doubt Todd dropped in at the house on the veld occasionally.

Mechanically she went about her work at the quarry site, but on Thursday evening she knew she couldn't put off a trip to Coult's any longer. The safari hunt was planned for the coming Sunday and he would want to discuss the arrangements with her. Also, though there was nothing to be gained from the chance meeting, still her foolish heart craved any opportunity to run into Todd.

She drove over to Coult's house, and arrived in time for dinner. Over the meal Coult told her that it had been decided to drive out to the Aasvogel Arena at dawn on Sunday and camp out until the following morning so that the men would have time to get their money's worth out of the licence fees.

Later, sipping drinks on the veranda, Rennie wondered how she could broach the subject closest to her heart. She knew she handled it clumsily, as twirling her glass she asked lightly, 'Had any visitors lately?'

'Nope.' Coult looked past her to the dark outdoors. 'Todd's not here.'

'Not here?' Rennie echoed his words a little faintly.

'He's gone to Johannesburg.'

She made an effort not to slump in her chair as she asked, 'To see Lila?'

'That's right.' Coult screwed the cap on the wine bottle.

A little while later Rennie left. She had made the excuse that she needed an early night, but though her eyes smarted as she drove back to the bungalow it was not through lack of sleep. She couldn't stay at Vukasi. She would have to leave ... go right away. Back to England perhaps, or some-

where far away from Africa ... and Todd. After the safari
trip she would tell Coult that she couldn't accept his offer
of the mine.

While Rennie got through the days in quiet despair life
around the settlement was going with a swing. There were
summer parties and evening outings to the river, and those
with older children up for the college vacation were enjoying happy family reunions. On Saturday she was invited
over to the Crowthers'. Jill, the couple's second daughter,
was celebrating her sixteenth birthday, and there was to
be a small gathering on the lawn.

Knowing that it was to be a casual affair Rennie dressed
in linen slacks and cotton blouse and drove up to the mine
manager's house in the afternoon. She had met the two
older daughters and made friends with them in a loose way
during her occasional visits to the Crowthers. She went
through into the girls' bedroom when she arrived, with a
small gift for Jill. The younger of the two was still at the
puppy fat stage, with a round smiling face and straight
fair hair. Her sister Patti, who was eighteen, was slim and
pretty and had very definite ideas about love and marriage.

'Leo's only five,' she said during the chat as they titivated
themselves at the mirror. 'I think it's disgusting to have
children in middle age. Mother and Father are ancient. I
shall have all my family before I'm twenty-five and become
celibate at thirty.'

Rennie sitting beside the dressing table drew in her
smile. 'You may change your mind when you're older,' she
said lightly. 'Having children late in life is supposed to keep
one young. Your mother and father are idyllically happy.'

'It's embarrassing coming home.' Patti swished her hair
before the mirror. 'I was horrified to discover that they still
sleep in the same bed.'

Later, while she was fastening a copper medallion round
her neck, she eyed Rennie curiously and asked, 'Will you

really own the whole mine one day? What are you going to do with all that money?'

'If it was me,' Jill whirled towards the door, 'I'd have a dress made entirely out of diamonds.'

'Silly! She'd get kidnapped the minute she went out.'

The girls laughed as they made for the garden, but Rennie felt the goose pimples rise on her skin. She was reminded of the mysterious notes she had been receiving, and to her the joke had a hollow ring.

The guests at the gathering were mainly young people. There were one or two close friends of the family and play-mates for the little Crowthers. Though Patti liked to appear airily grown up she secretly doted on her young brothers and sisters and spared a moment now and again to romp with them and play games. Jill was the star of the show. It wasn't every day one was sixteen. She proudly handed around slices of birthday cake and chose the music for the record player. Rennie made an effort to blend in with the gaiety. Like Patti she joined in the children's games. Baby Leo was her favourite partner. He wasn't so discerning as the grown-ups. With him she didn't have to worry that her laughter didn't ring true.

At one point he became a little too rough and excitable and she left him to his own devices for a while. Some time later she heard his shout of laughter near the gate. She turned, and her heart catapulted into her throat. Todd was swinging young Leo up as he moved across the lawn. So he was back!

Over by the drinks table Rennie felt faint at the sight of him. He was wearing pale slacks and a dark open-necked shirt. The Crowther children climbed over him. Jill gave a squeal when she saw him. 'Todd! What have you brought me?' She ran to throw her arms round his neck, gigglingly trying to discover what he held behind his back.

'Lucky!' Patti, smiling up at Todd, was scathingly envious of her sister's favoured position. Rennie, looking on, swallowed painfully. She was aware that Todd knew everyone at the mine, but she didn't know that he was on such familiar terms with the Crowthers' college daughters.

He came over to the drinks table and accepted the things that the girls stuffed into his hands. 'Hello, young Rennie.' He slanted her a green glance over the top of his slab of birthday cake. 'Enjoying yourself?'

'It's a wonderful party,' she replied lightly. She wanted to die. Todd passed on and went to talk with Sylvia and Martin, sitting in deck chairs at the front of the house.

The afternoon had been bearable before; now Rennie moved among the other guests choking back the misery inside her and praying for the time when she could decently make an exit. She battled it out smilingly, mainly as an onlooker. The record player churned out the music. Patti, in dreamy frame of mind, called pleadingly, 'Todd, dance with me.'

Indulgently he joined her where the other young couples were gyrating. The beat was powerful, the music fluid. Patti had an uninhibited style, and so as it turned out had Todd. Rennie watched his relaxed frame moving flowingly to the beat. She was both fascinated and in an abyss of unhappiness. She felt a stab of pain when he drew the young figure close and swayed with her in conventional style. Was he dancing like this with Patti to forget Lila?

It seemed as though the party would never break up, but at last the food and drink on the table was depleted, the chatter and laughter died down, and people started drifting away. Rennie said goodbye to the young Crowthers. When she left Todd was talking to Martin near the house. At least that was the way it looked, so she was a little startled to discover a couple of minutes later as she was making her way out to her range truck, that Todd was coming up leisurely behind her.

'Thought I'd better come out and check that my car's not blocking your way,' he said easily.

It was true the shoulder of the road was narrow, but she had plenty of room to pull away. She couldn't think why he had bothered.

'Great family, the Crowthers,' he said, following her out.

'The envy of most of the settlement, I would think.' Trying to sound equally casual, she replied with hardly a tremor in her voice.

'Oh, I don't know. I've an idea that as many as five children is looked down upon by some of our more élite neighbours,' Todd said opening the gate.

'It depends on the couple,' Rennie pointed out a little tightly. 'Some are happy with a brood. Others take just as well to a pair of pekingese.'

'I guess you're right.' Todd propped himself up against the flowering hedge, his green gaze openly searching.

'Anyway,' with forced gaiety Rennie couldn't resist a little succinct humour, 'when the daughters are grown up they soon come back into popularity.'

Todd must have known what she was hinting at. He said, his gaze still on her, 'Patti will make someone a good wife some day.'

'I'm sure she will.' Her voice sounded horribly high-pitched. Why couldn't she get away? Why did she have to stay here and wring her heart in her hands? Through her brittle gaiety Todd seemed to be raking her mind, her innermost feelings with his eyes. She turned at last and reached for the handle of the truck door. She was just going to step jauntily inside when something fluttered to the ground. *Another note!* At the sight of it she stopped breathing. It must have been hidden there somewhere in the door. Perhaps she had missed it earlier when she had driven over here.

Todd said with a tight grin, 'What's this? A secret admirer?' And at her scared look, 'Well, read what the guy says. Could be he's too shy to ask for a date.'

Rennie read the note automatically. Perhaps she swayed a little, for Todd asked abruptly, 'What is it? What's wrong? You look frightened out of your wits.'

She tried to pass the matter off lightly. 'Oh, it's just some crank having his little joke.' But Todd said sharply,

'Let me see that.'

The message still burned before Rennie's eyes.

You're pushing your luck hanging on at the mine. If you want to leave on your feet you'd better get out while you can.

Todd read the note grimly. 'Nice character,' he said through a clamped jaw. And to Rennie, 'Have you received other notes besides this?'

'Oh, a couple!' she said airily, tossing them on to the car seat from her pocket. She had kept them mainly to compare the handwriting.

Todd read them, and his face became more set as he growled, 'I've a feeling this joker means business.'

Rennie climbed into the truck and closed the door. 'I hardly think so,' she replied lightly. 'I'm sure it's just someone looking for a little diverse amusement.'

'With you as the moving target,' Todd snapped. Something seemed to click in his mind as he spoke. His arm on the open window, he said, looking at her sharply, 'And tomorrow you're going on the safari with Coult.'

Rennie started up and laughed her brittle laugh. 'I'm looking forward to the trip,' she lied blithely. 'And I'm sure you're making mountains out of molehills. Who could possibly be interested in stirring up trouble for me?' She pulled out into the road. She was only concerned with getting away before he saw through her strained merriment to the raging heartache beneath.

As she gave him a brief wave Todd tapped the notes thoughtfully in his hand and said grimly, watching her go, 'That's what I'd like to know.'

It was later in the evening at the mine owner's house when Rennie learned that Todd had changed his mind and was coming on the safari after all. She drove back to her bungalow for the night unmoved by the news. What difference did it make? Todd didn't love her. He had probably only agreed to come on the trip under pressure from Coult.

CHAPTER THIRTEEN

THE hunting party gathered out on the hill settlement road at dawn the following morning. The mine executives had borrowed sturdy company vehicles for the trek, and most had a cook boy along. Coult had brought Aaron plus Romaano the gardener to help out with the chores. There was a slight pantomime before they got settled in the Landrover. Coult, with a subtle gleam in his eye, waved Rennie magnanimously ahead of him. 'Sit up front girl, next to Todd. Get the best view. Me and the boys can make ourselves comfortable in the back.'

Rennie took her seat dutifully next to Todd at the wheel, painfully aware of his damp, early morning freshness, and the crisp, starchy fragrance of his khaki shirt and slacks. She was wearing a similar outfit. Leaving the river road, the car convoy aimed for the sandstone bluffs, blobs of grape blue in the misty dawn light. The veld had the open look of parkland. The feathery foliage of the terminalia trees stirred in the first cool breezes. There were bushveld willows and sometimes palms in the dry watercourses.

Coming up to the entrance between the towering bluffs, Coult said from behind, 'We figured that the mud flats over to the east would be a good place to pitch the tents, Todd. It will be cool there and we'll have Skelm rise at our backs for protection.'

'I know the place,' Todd nodded. Their vehicle was in front as he led the way into the Aasvogel Arena. Rennie was familiar with some of the woodland paths and game trails. She made an effort to show an interest in their route for Coult's sake. He didn't know she was leaving Vukasi. She swallowed on the lump in her throat. She would tell him as soon as they got back from the safari.

They came to a halt at the chosen spot and pitched the tents at the foot of a high escarpment. Before them were the mud flats, catchment areas for mountain rains. A chain of pools mirrored the reflection of surrounding bush and trees. The vehicles were parked in the shade of trees and the men spent the time perfecting their weapons and wallowing in the freedom of camp life. They planned to rest and start out on foot in the early afternoon.

Around midday the fragrance of cooking wafted through the bush. Coult was enjoying himself. As they sat on their camp stools tin plates in their hands he said matily, smacking his lips, 'I sure am glad you decided to come on the trip, Todd.' And with a sly look in her direction, 'And Rennie's glad too, ain't ya, girl?'

Over by the cooking fire she replied primly, 'Of course it's nice to have Todd with us.' She avoided the green gaze across the clearing, tears at the back of her throat. Coult meant well. He didn't know that he was wasting his time.

Todd said, taking up his mug of coffee, 'It's great to be out in the open.'

It was later when she was helping to clear the things away that Rennie received a nasty jolt. She went to recover the things she had used for her meal and there in the handle of the mug that she had left in the grass was a rolled-up note.

The blood drained from her veins. *So it was someone here.* Quickly she looked around. The scene was normal. The men were moving about checking their gear for the afternoon trek. There was keyed-up laughter and backslapping and testing out the weight of packs. Todd, who was going over his and Coult's rifles, had the whole camp in his view.

Rennie bent to retrieve the mug and swiftly smoothed out the note. The words danced up at her from between the blades of grass.

Perhaps we can talk this thing over. When you've read this drive to the burning bush on the main plain. There's an uprooted tree. Meet me there on foot.

Rennie knew the place where the tangle of blood red flowers made a beacon about a mile inside the arena entrance. She screwed the note in her hand and rose. She didn't want to spoil things for Coult, and perhaps he would never know. She could be there and back in a few minutes if she could get hold of some transport. Besides—her lips tightened imperceptibly as she moved over to the washing-up bowl—it would be good to meet her tormentor face to face and put an end to this business once and for all.

From the washing-up area she slid away through the trees and worked her way round to where the vehicles were parked. It was tricky trying to decide which one to take. Several of the men were doing jobs nearby. Realising that she couldn't afford to waste time, she took a deep breath and smilingly approached the chief in administration. 'Can I borrow your truck, Frank? I want to make a little trip.'

Frank Markson, big and red-faced, frowned up from polishing his field glasses. 'This isn't the kind of place to go driving alone.' He eyed her keenly. 'Shouldn't you have someone along?'

'Oh, I'll only be a few minutes. There's some flowers I want to pick for Coult. It's perfectly safe.' She must have sounded convincing, for he nodded his head reluctantly.

'Well, okay. But don't be long.'

She was in the truck and crunching silently through the trees before he could change his mind. Once out on the track she sped over the ground. Luckily she was familiar now with the different routes in the arena and it wasn't long before she had left the mud flats behind and was speeding towards the burning bush out there on the plain. In a way she thanked her mysterious messenger for choosing such a spot. In the tangled bushveld there was the ever-present danger of running into animals—wasn't the place bursting at the seams with herds of wild game?—but out in the open one could keep an eye open for trouble.

Where the towering bluffs stood out against the hot blue sky, the outer veld and distant horizons framed in their entrance like a giant canvas, she pulled in and left the truck in a shallow gulley out of sight. She walked over to the burning bush, a copse of tangled flowers where green flies buzzed in the heat and tree cicadas clicked monotonously. There was no one around.

She shaded her eyes searching the landscape and drew on her lower lip when she saw something which resembled an uprooted tree in the distance. What should she do? It would take her a while to reach it. All things being normal nothing would have induced her to go wandering alone across the African veld. But her mind and wits were dulled by unhappiness. She was in a suspended state where she didn't particularly care what lay ahead. All she wanted to do was meet the writer of the notes face to face.

Slackly she moved across the turf. Behind her were the encircling forests and shimmering bushveld. To right and left, hilly ramparts of rose-red granite rocks merged in with the sandstone ridges which made the bottleneck pass out through the twin bluffs.

It was a scene of primitive grandeur, but it was lost on Rennie. She was aware only of the shrill sound of the cicadas, of how the haze made an illusory marsh of the thirsty grassland, and of the sigh of the wind spilling over the edges of the ridges. Everywhere was crackling heat.

She had been walking for some time before she became conscious of a very distinctive crackling, a sound that had nothing to do with the sun's rays on the parched grass. She turned and was vaguely alarmed to see a tremendous amount of smoke back there in the forest. Even as she watched huge flames licked upwards and she realised, her tongue drying against the roof of her mouth, that the whole bush was on fire.

Rooted to the spot, she had no idea what to do. Would the fire travel in this direction? If it did where would she go, stranded out in the open as she was? This new peril jerking her awake to the crazy vulnerability of her position she wondered whether she should keep going or turn back.

It was while she was deciding to abandon her attempts to discover the identity of the writer of the threatening notes and make for safety that she saw with a stab of horror that the fire was the least of her worries. Heat and flames have a devastating effect on tinder-dry woodland, sending everything fleeing from its path, and surging out into view now, drawing ever nearer on wave upon wave of dust, was the thunder of fear-crazed animals racing for safety. Rennie glanced wildly around her. And there was only one way out —through the bottleneck pass behind her.

What could she do? Even if she had the strength to run there was nowhere to go, not so much as a hummock on the grassy plain to hide behind. White and shaking, she tried to make some decision, but her brain was stupefied with terror. The flames were licking behind and through a pall of smoke and dust spreading out across the grassland she could see the horned creatures racing head down in blind panic, see the soaring, leaping, terrified shapes of smaller animals, and though she didn't want to believe it she could smell the fear of the galloping, thundering advancing stampede.

As she stood hypnotised with horror, glued there in the path of the approaching holocaust, the words of the threatening note came crazily to her mind: *accidents can happen—accidents can happen*. Hysteria rose in her throat. She could feel the grit of the dust on her lips, hear the ground-trembling thud of the nearing hooves.

A small dot in the path of a tidal wave of plunging flesh, she heard the scream climbing in her throat. It rose and broke on the air as a sob of hope as she stared ahead. *Could it be? It was!* Coult's Landrover racing over the smouldering grass. Bouncing, hurtling, speeding through and ahead of the thundering stampede. It was Todd at the wheel, Todd fighting to wring every ounce of speed out of the Landrover. But he was only yards ahead of the pall of dust, yards that shrank to feet as he neared her. Rennie could see the chiselled strain on his face. Sods of earth flew up at her from the oncoming flying hooves. *Todd wouldn't reach her. He couldn't do it.* She saw the blaze of encouragement in his eyes. She was sinking to her knees. A numbness spread over, and then wonderfully, miraculously, he was holding her. He had slewed to a halt and flung her to the ground with him in the shelter of the Landrover before she had time to come out of her daze.

For the next few minutes, which seemed like a lifetime, they huddled beneath the furore above them. Stifled against Todd's protective frame, Rennie listened to the steady thunder, to the ring of hoof against metal as fear-crazed beasts leapt and slithered over the Landrover, to the voiceless, frantic rhythm of animals fleeing to safety.

They were showered with earth, with rocks, with gravel, although Rennie's only discomfort was the weight of Todd's body moulding her with him against the side of the truck. She thought she would have to struggle up for air and then suddenly the thunder passed on, it faded rapidly leaving a dust-filled stillness. A glance in that direction showed the thudding exodus making for the twin bluffs. Back towards the bush the smoke had died down. Todd croaked, 'The wind's blowing the fire towards the mud flats. It will burn itself out.'

Slowly coming to he sat up and jerked Rennie with him.

Anger and relief mingled in his gaze as he looked at her and exploded through clenched teeth, shaking her roughly. 'I ought to break your neck for coming out here alone when you know someone's got a grudge against you over the diamond mine.'

Her hair tumbling about her face, Rennie snapped back, 'I'm sick of the whole business! I wish Coult had never made me his heir. I don't want the diamond mine, and I mean to tell him so after the safari.'

Todd looked into her face. He was probing, searching again. He said, watching her, 'There's no need to be frightened. We can put a stop to those threats.'

'It's not that.' She lowered her gaze.

'What is it, then?' His fingers were sinking into the flesh of her shoulders. He willed her to meet his gaze.

She lifted her eyes and choked, slumping against him, 'Oh, Todd! I'm so unhappy.'

'Does this help a little?' He put a finger under her chin and raising it placed his lips gently on hers.

'Help?' Rennie gasped, starry-eyed. 'It's the answer to everything!'

'You're sure you won't mind being plain Mrs Dillman?' So that was it! Todd had no wish to compete with a diamond mine. *It wasn't Lila after all!* Her spirits soared to an overwhelming joy and she said softly against him, 'Mind! It's all I want in the world.'

He kissed her again, hungrily yet tenderly and oh, so lingeringly.

To still her wildly beating heart she asked a long time later, 'How did you know where I'd gone?'

'I didn't,' he replied grimly. 'I went through hell trying to find you. Frank Markson got worried when you didn't come back and I tore him off a strip for letting you go. I used the field glasses from the escarpment. I saw the fire first. From there I spotted you wandering on your own across the veld.'

Rennie shuddered. 'I received another note in the camp. That's why I came out here.'

'I've been thinking about that.' Todd drew up a knee and rested an arm on it thoughtfully. 'Hasn't Coult got a relative, a cousin or something in Johannesburg?'

Rennie nodded. 'You think it's him behind the trouble?' She sat a little straighter.

'It has to be,' Todd nodded. 'That kind of news travels fast. I'd like to bet he's been operating on the spot somewhere nearby in Wykveld. He must have bribed someone to deliver the notes. Someone who knows you fairly well.'

Rennie pondered and then snapped her fingers. 'Romaano! He knows where my bungalow is. He goes to Wykveld to buy plants for the gardens, and he's here with the safari today.' She frowned. 'But he wouldn't have started the fire.'

'No,' Todd said tightly. 'The cousin would want to handle that himself. I've no doubt he'd make certain of saving his own neck before the blaze.'

'What will happen to him?' Rennie asked soberly.

'He'll be caught and punished,' came the harsh reply.

She looked back to where the smoke was drifting fitfully in the distance and asked worriedly, 'What about Coult and the others?'

'The camp will be safe on the mud flats. If I know Coult he'll have used my look-out and spotted us out here. It'll take a while for the ground to cool. We'll go back later.' He drew her close to him. 'Much later.'

Rennie looked a little downcast. 'Coult's going to be hurt when I tell him I don't want his money,' she sighed.

'Somehow I don't think he will be,' came the soft reply. 'He's been to see me a lot these last few days and he talked about you all the time.' Todd grinned. 'Coult has no finesse when it comes to matters of the heart. I think he had an idea that the diamond mine had come between us.'

Rennie had sensed that too and she had the feeling that Coult was watching them now and smirking with satisfaction. She said with a bright thought,' As no real harm's been done perhaps the cousin might come back into favour one day?'

'That we shall have to wait and see,' Todd said sternly. And then with a low laugh, 'Hey, how about a few pre-wife touches around here? I could do with a wash and there should be some drinks in the truck.'

'Yes, my lord.' Laughing happily, Rennie rose and set about making a few home comforts. In a bowl of fresh water Todd stripped off his shirt and washed away the dust and smoke soot. Afterwards Rennie rinsed off and brushed out her hair. She spread a car rug on the coarse grass and brought glasses and a few picnic items from the truck's supply. The sun dropped behind the ridge and the veld was bathed in a restful gloom. Red and gold finches glided close to the ground and flashing honey birds flew up from the red granite rocks.

Nestled close to Todd as they sat propped against the truck wheel, she said with the wheedlings of a woman, 'Tell me about Lila.'

'There's nothing to tell,' he shrugged. 'She's always been in love with Pete, but she couldn't get him to see things her way. She thought the answer was to start an affair with me, so I played along. It seemed a good way to get them both to see sense. Then you mucked things up a little.' He grinned wryly.

'You mean that night at the mine anniversary party?' Rennie bit on her smile.

Todd nodded. 'It was okay for Lila to fool around, but she saw red when she thought Peter was falling for you. That's when she went off the rails.'

Rennie asked with concern, 'Will she get better?'

'She's improving daily,' Todd smiled. 'And under Peter's care she'll be able to lead a fairly normal life. They're getting married soon. I think Lila's seen that a doctor's job is a pretty important one.'

Rennie mused on this and asked a little sadly. 'What will happen to Rosedale now?'

Todd took a breath and with a lopsided grin he said, 'Coult will probably murder me for telling you this. He was keeping it as a surprise. He's bought Rosedale.'

'He has?' Rennie gasped, shining-eyed, and then at Todd, 'Is that why you went down to see Lila?'

He nodded. 'Coult wanted to make sure that she had no further interest in it. He approached her father, who was only too glad to sell.'

'So you'll still be beautifying the grounds,' Rennie sighed happily.

'More than ever now,' Todd replied. 'Coult has very definite ideas what he wants. He plans to live there when the deal's gone through.'

Rennie thought of the lovely old house and grounds and looking up at him she said with a penitent gleam, 'I did tease you about your job, didn't I?'

'I was pretty insufferable myself,' he admitted, trailing his lips through her hair. 'You got under my skin from that very first day. You were so damned dedicated to your profession. I became insanely jealous of the priority you gave it ... of Leith mauling you with his great beefy hands ...'

'And speaking of jealousies,' Rennie said innocently, tracing his lips with her finger, 'what about only as recently as yesterday and you dancing with Patti Crowther?'

'I was wishing it was you in my arms.' He brushed his lips across her nose.

'Of course, you couldn't have told me that,' she said with ironic humour.

'I didn't see myself married to a diamond mine heiress,' he shrugged.

'Do you see yourself married to an engineer?' she twinkled.

'Nope. I fell in love with a girl called Spring. She wears frilly dresses and moves like a dream.' His lips moved playfully over hers and he murmured, 'For me it will always be spring.'

'Daddy will have a fit,' Rennie suppressed a giggle.

'He'll get over it,' came the lazy reply.

'He really did want me to be like him,' she sighed. 'But I think the dynamite episode put an end to it.'

Todd gripped her close. 'I wanted to send you a million miles away from the danger that night, but I knew you'd never consent to go, and there was no time to do it by force.'

'I wouldn't have gone,' she shook her head firmly. 'And you handled it superbly.'

'I held your life in my hands.' He gazed down at her. 'I couldn't afford any slip-ups.'

Secure in his arms, she said after a while on a humorous note, 'Do I have to share you with the settlement wives?'

'We'll do our duty and drop in on the odd party once in a while,' he smiled. 'But most of the time we'll be pretty secluded out by the airstrip. And then there's our honeymoon. I want to show you South Africa—the lovely Cape Peninsular, sub-tropical Natal, the Garden Route and the Dutch homesteads and vineyards.'

It sounded heavenly, and in her happiness Rennie was reminded of another young recruit to the country. 'By the way,' she looked up at him, 'Darrell says he's going to write to you from Johannesburg. I suppose he'll be under Peter's wing at the hospital.'

Todd shrugged. 'You seemed to have a soft spot for the kid, so I felt obliged to help.'

'You've got a soft spot too.' She eyed him with an accusing twinkle. 'I happen to know that you were bending over backwards to help Darrell before I arrived on the scene.'

'There's hope for our kids, then,' he grinned. And with an idle twinkle back at her, 'What will you do if your father comes out in one of them?'

'Not to worry,' she said lightly. 'We'll just put him out to train as a brilliant engineer.' Noses together, they laughed wickedly.

From her side of the Landrover Rennie could see the slowly dispersing smoke. She said with concern, 'The fire will be a blow to the safari.'

'There'll be another day,' Todd replied easily. 'And think of the animals running away scot free.'

'Now there's a nice thought!' She lay back in his arms and as she stared into space she was blissfully content. Somewhere up there, beyond the blue, was the brightest star. Hers and Todd's.

We hope you have enjoyed this romance.
Mills & Boon publish Ten Romances
each month, all of which are of the same
high standard.
Don't be disappointed — place a standing
order for Mills & Boon titles without delay.

191

Choose from this selection of

Mills & Boon

Golden Treasury
COLLECTION

☐ **GT1**
GOLDEN APPLE ISLAND
Jane Arbor

☐ **GT2**
CARPET OF DREAMS
Susan Barrie

☐ **GT3**
UNTIL THE HEART WILLS (Nurse Rita)
Lucy Bowdler

☐ **GT4**
A RING ON HER FINGER
Mary Burchell

☐ **GT5**
THE BAY OF MOONLIGHT
Rose Burghley

☐ **GT6**
THE LAND OF THE LOTUS-EATERS
Isobel Chace

☐ **GT7**
A TASTE FOR LOVE
Joyce Dingwell

☐ **GT8**
TO TAKE HEART (Scatterbrains, Student Nurse)
Margaret Malcolm

☐ **GT9**
BY CANDELIGHT
Sara Seale

☐ **GT10**
THE LARK IN THE MEADOW
Essie Summers

*Readers in Australia, New Zealand, South Africa and Rhodesia please refer to Order Form overleaf for special details of local addresses, prices, postage costs, Etc.